THE FILTHY ONE

THE ESCORT SERIES VOLUME 3

N.O. ONE

THE FILTHY ONE

WARNING / FOREWORD

Before you continue...

The Filthy One is the third volume of a series of six.

It is graphic and morally on the fence, containing extremely sensitive material that may not be adapted to your needs.

If you need specific details of things involved, please visit our website for a list of warnings.

www.author-no-one.com

If you're okay with all of this, just remember... we warned you.

On the plus side, the lead female is strong and proud and these men come with a fire extinguisher.

If you're still reading after all of that then, by all means, sit down, relax, and enjoy the filthy, bumpy road ahead.

To reiterate:

!! If you have triggers, please do not continue. This is not the series for you. !!

Seriously, if you don't want all the angst and smut with some suspenseful darkness thrown in for good measure, stop reading.

Did you stop?

No?

Excellent! You're now one of us and we have claimed
you as our own, you filthy rebel you ;)

Ray Liotta

Chapter One
River

"I like to have control." My gaze darts up to the man sitting right across from me, the fancy coffee shop set-up looks like someone's Park Avenue living room, even with a sex contract lying on the table.

I smirk.

"Don't we all?" It takes him a second to move from his relaxed position to that of a coiled cobra ready to strike. Intense gray eyes pierce right through me as he sits up, elbows resting on the slacks of his midnight-blue Ford suit, and clasps his hands together as though needing to hold himself back.

"No. Some want the illusion of control. Others willingly give it away. I'm neither of those. I have control because I take it. Do you understand what I'm saying?" I don't answer right away, letting this information settle between us before I add it all to my notes.

"And in this scenario, am I giving you control or am I pretending to have it?" With one brow raised in defiance, I let him know that I'm not begging for his business. I don't need him to sign this contract, I can live without his money. In fact, the only reason I'm even considering him is because I need to keep myself busy. And by busy, I mean I need to keep my mind from constantly going back to Nathaniel and wondering why I'm paying for the sins of others. I've tried contacting him, I've sent text messages—our usual banter—but he hasn't responded. Not once. I get it, he's protecting his heart. But in doing so, he's breaking mine.

So, here I am, diving into my work and hoping this guy is merely looking for candy on his arm at his multiple functions. After all, Tyler Walker sent him my way so chances are, I'll be getting paid for looking pretty and smiling.

"Hmm, I suppose that's for you to choose. Ultimately, I make all the decisions. Where we eat. Where we sleep. How we fuck and for how long. I decide what you do or don't wear, how you speak and to whom. And when we fuck, I decide which hole I take and how hard I take it." With a shrug, he sits back into the chair, resuming his position of false relaxation.

There goes the arm-candy theory.

I have a feeling this man is anything but calm. In fact, I'm seriously considering refusing his business even though the slight accent intrigues me. Definitely a bit of Brooklyn but there's something more to it. The lilt of a song and a rolling of his consonants.

"Let's be clear, here. Your control reaches as far as the words on this contract. Not a letter more. We will discuss your terms and then I will lay out my hard limits. If this arrangement does not agree with you, then I think it's best we end this conversation right now." I stand, flicking the deep brown strand of my wig off my shoulder and stare down at him while he contemplates my words.

It's the wild fucking west as his pensive stare roams my face, dancing from one eye to the other, over my lips and back up to my eyes. He's testing me, wondering if I'll cower at his eerie silence. What he doesn't know is that men like him, in my business, are a dime a dozen. Control freaks who think hiring an escort gives them the right to treat us like their own personal blow-up doll.

Yeah, I don't think so.

Slowly, a faint smile forms at the corners of his mouth as he pulls one cuff, then the other, before crossing his leg over his knee and sitting like a king on his fucking throne.

"I like you. You'll do quite nicely." His gaze moves from me to the seat I had occupied only seconds ago. "Please, sit. Let's try this again, shall we?" I watch him, reading his every move, every tick he may have. In my profession, you have to go with your gut. And your research, of course. Except, I haven't had time to do my due diligence yet. All I have is the name I was given from a sweet-sounding receptionist as a referral from Tyler with the address to this coffee shop only a couple of hours before my meeting time.

When he sees me hesitate, he rises to his feet, takes one step closer to me and holds out his hand.

This is it, I think. I'm either on board or walking away.

Problem is, I'm curious as fuck and when he tilts his head to the side and flashes me a smile that lights up his entire olive-tinted skin and I realize there's no turning back. I need to know more.

"Let's try this again."

Holding out my hand, we shake once before he introduces himself properly, his impressive stature erasing everything around me.

"Marco Mancini, at your service."

CHAPTER TWO
RIVER

"Now that we have the introductions out of the way, let's focus on the logistics, shall we?"

Carefully placing my Mont Blanc fountain pen on the stack of papers, I cross my legs at the knees, making sure I don't give him a peek at the goods. "I'm listening."

At the ripe old age of twenty-six, I've been an escort for the better part of eight years. At first, I just needed the money so I could take care of my brother and make sure he got the best education, the world was his oyster and all that shit. Thanks to Polly, I learned a few tricks along the way.

The most useful of those tricks being how to read a room. More specifically, to read the john. Of course, I'm not cheap. I'm not walking the streets for just enough cash to get through the night, thank fuck. I got lucky when I met Polly, never had to fuck for scraps. If I could, I'd build my own brothel and make this a job with dignity. I mean, our sexuality is sold for everything else, why not for our own profit with our own rules?

But that's a fight for another time.

Right now, I have this confident, too handsome for his own good, mob boss wannabe piercing me with his gray eyes and trying to assess me the same way I'm trying to read him.

No doubt he's got enough money to set up his great-grand-children. The sex appeal is off the charts. The dominant gene did not skip over him, either. The trifecta of the New York elite: rich, sexy, confident.

"I need a wife and you're perfect for the job." Believe it or not, this isn't the first time I've been propositioned for this particular job offer.

"Not interested." I refuse to get tied down into someone else's world. I've got my family to worry about, I can't be at some total stranger's finicky whim.

"You haven't heard my proposal." The subtle chuckle under his breath paired with the uptick of one corner of his mouth, tells me he's amused by my refusal. Probably thinks I'm playing hard to get.

I'm not.

"I'm glad to hear that because as proposals go, that one was subpar. I'm sure any of the Upper East Side debutants would be thrilled, though." I lean in and whisper like it's the best kept secret in New York. "It's still a no for me." Uncrossing my legs and gathering up my documents for what has turned out to be a great big waste of my time, I look up and find him watching me intently. A shiver runs down the length of my spine and it has nothing to do with fear. Those eyes are magnetic and if I were any other woman, living any other life, I'd be stupid to say no to this man. I'm guessing he's planning on offering an obscene amount of money, too. Except, how much could it actually be worth, this fake wedding? A hundred thousand? I could make that in two months if I choose my clients well.

Plus, I'm still reeling from the whole Nathaniel ordeal. His last words both hurt and pissed me off.

"When your heart finally decides who it wants to belong to, you know where to find me. Or him."

Why is it we're always paying for the mistakes of others? Kai has been in my life for as long as I can remember. I don't know a time when I didn't love him, but that doesn't change the fact that I didn't deserve the ultimatum. Not to mention the choice is no longer in my hands. Freya may have been a cunt to me, but that's not who I am. He's engaged, case closed.

"I get down on my knees for no one, but I can say this. Five million. Two tonight, three at the end of our contract. Three months, beginning to end." Smug, with a smirk that tells a story of privilege and the absence of the word "no" thrown at his face, he leans back and waits for me to fall at his feet.

When I thought he'd propose an obscene amount of money, I was not expecting that. And as much as I would love to say yes without a second thought—the money would change my life, not to mention my brother's—for all I know, he expects equally obscene things from me.

"Hmm, you drive a hard bargain, Mr. Mancini. Let me hear your... what did you call them? Logistics?" It can't hurt to at least hear him out.

Checking his watch like this meeting is beginning to bore him, he straightens right before he rises to his feet and holds out a hand for me.

"Let's talk business over dinner." His hand outstretched, he arches a brow, eyes swimming in humor like he thinks I'm being cute.

"Look, you're very..."—I swirl a finger around his whole sexy mafia thing he's got going on—"pretty. And frankly, quite sexy, but it's barely three in the afternoon and I have other potential clients I need to meet." Sweeping all of my papers into my leather satchel, I rise to my feet and scowl at the height difference between us. Even in my heels, he's towering over me, making me feel small and insignificant.

Except, that look in his eyes says otherwise.

He wants me.

"All of your meetings have been canceled." I frown, trying to register the words that just came out of his mouth. Then I laugh, my head thrown back like he's the new stand-up comedian of the century.

Sighing, I look back at him and find he's not the least bit amused.

"Wait, are you serious?" *What the actual fucking fuck?* Blinking away the shock of what he's just admitted, I scoff, but there's exactly zero humor in it.

"You can't be serious." Taking out my phone, I bring up the calendar app and notice all of my appointments, four of them today and two tomorrow, have been canceled. I keep staring at the screen like somehow it will come back up and this is all a misunderstanding. Except the days and hours stay completely empty.

"How…?"

"I have a guy."

He… has a guy? What the fuck does that even mean?

"You can't do that!" I reel in my suddenly-loud voice, remembering where I am, and whisper-yell at him, putting all of my indignation into each of my words. "Who the fuck do you think you are, invading my privacy like that?" We're nose to nose—as much as possible given the height difference—eyes boring into each other. My nostrils are flaring, my entire body buzzing with pent-up anger while Mr. Sex-in-a-Suit almost looks bored with this entire exchange.

"I like to eliminate my competition." He shrugs, barely affected by our altercation.

"Un-fucking-believable." Throwing my hands up, I take a step back ready to leave him behind and let him deal with his own predicament.

"Watch your language. I expect my wife to speak elegantly and not like a whore off the streets." He bends low enough for his next words to be just for me. "Unless my dick is buried so deep inside her that sophistication is fucked right out of her. Only then, do I approve."

The fucking gall of this guy.

"Well then, it's settled." Our faces are so close right now, I can feel his minty breath caress my parted lips. "Fuck, shit, and cunt are my favorite words in the English repertoire. And, Mr. Mancini? I change for no man." With a raised brow, I give him my sweetest smile before turning on my heel and taking my first step away from him.

The slight hint of vanilla and spice is the only warning I get as his hand latches onto my bicep, his chest flush against my back as his lips graze my outer ear. "You have twenty-four hours to pack your bags, River Fox. I will send my car and the driver will let you know when he's arrived. You will get into the car with one suitcase for whatever is absolutely necessary. The rest I will provide for you."

My heart is beating in my throat, my anger so present inside me it's like a living, breathing thing. He fucking knows my real name. Right now, I want to beat the crap out of "his guy."

But I am in control of my emotions and refuse to lose my shit. Taking in a deep, and much needed breath, I slowly turn so I'm face to face with this dark, fucking gorgeous specimen of a man and smile.

We only met all of thirty minutes ago, but at the sight of the robotic upturn of my lips, his brows pinch, his delicious looking mouth turning upside down. We don't know each other but he's not an idiot. He fucking knows I'm about to go off on him.

"Twenty-four hours?" Cocking my head to the side, I ask for confirmation.

It takes him a few seconds to answer, not expecting me to be so docile. I'm sure he can tell something just isn't right.

"Yes." Wary, he inspects every inch of my face with his laser-sharp eyes. "This time tomorrow, I want you ready."

I nod, as though in agreement, and take a step forward. This time, I'm the one invading his space, my lips almost grazing his inviting mouth.

"In twenty-four hours, you come to my residence and you will find that I will absolutely not be there. Do you know why? Because you, sir, can go fuck yourself. Repeatedly." This time, I turn and walk right out the coffee shop door.

Fucking hell, that felt incredible. I'm not twenty feet away when my phone buzzes in my hand. With a victorious grin on my face, I look down and see an unknown number.

Fuck, not again. These calls need to stop. But then, maybe it's one of my clients saying he's changed his mind and would like to meet me.

"Hello?"

"I'll be there at three-thirty-three, River Fox. And when I pull up, you'll wish you'd followed my instructions. See you tomorrow, *Dolcezza*."

My steps falter, my entire body buzzing with something I can't quite understand. Excitement? Fear? Anger. I settle on anger because out of every emotion swirling inside, it is the dominant one.

A quick search for the word he used at the end tells me it's a term of endearment, like sweet.

Sweet?

Ugh, I hate this asshole.

Then, I think about the five million dollars and wonder if turning it down is the height of stupidity.

I call him back. This time, steel in my voice.

"Yes, *Dolcezza*?"

"Fine. Dinner. I haven't agreed to the contract but I will listen to your terms, then I'll give you mine."

"Hmmm, I accept your invitation. I'll pick you up at seven." He hangs up and I try not to wonder how in the fuck he knows where I live.

CHAPTER THREE

RIVER

The pure and utter audacity of this man. One of those clients his so-called *guy* canceled for me this afternoon was a politician, and they always pay really well for little work. They think paying more ensures their secrecy. Not that I would ever break a contract like that with a client, but fuck me, it would've made up for losing Tyler and Elijah.

Still, there's no way in hell I'll be taking the job with Marco Mancini. *What kind of macho bullshit name is that anyway?* He's an overbearing, controlling, egotistical jerk-off. A jerk-off who's found a way to crawl under my skin and irritate me like no other.

Marriage just isn't something I can do, it'd take a hell of a lot more explaining to my family, for starters. After everything that went down with Nathaniel and Kai at Ev's, they'd probably see a sudden out-of-the-blue marriage as a cry for help.

Curiosity is the only reason I've agreed to dinner, mostly. I feel like I need to know why a man that looks as good as he does needs to pay for a wife. There's no doubt in my mind that he has the hottest women falling at his feet. But then again, maybe they all ran off the moment he opened that goddamn mouth of his.

A car horn coming from outside pulls me from my thoughts, making me jump a little, before I walk over to the window to see what's going on.

Of fucking course his car isn't discreet. I may be pretty dumb when it comes to vehicles, but even I can see the sleek, deep-red sports car parked outside my apartment is an Aston Martin. My phone pings, and I pick it up to see a message from the man himself.

MM: You've got two minutes.

Two minutes, my ass. He can wait now. I'm ready to walk out of my apartment to meet him, but that text message makes me want to disobey him. So I do.

Checking myself over one more time in the floor-length mirror in my room, I run my hands over the smooth satin of my red pant suit. It's a bold choice, I know, but I love the way the wide pants allow just a peek at my Louboutin's, and how the jacket hugs my curves just right. It comes down in a V-shape to just between my breasts, showing the round globes off nicely with a whisper of my matching lacy bra. The chestnut brown wig I'm wearing is swept to the front in loose curls over one shoulder, framing my perfectly made-up face. Even if I do say so myself. My lipstick matches the suit and my eyes are dark and smoky, like my fucking mood when I'm around this man.

"I said two minutes."

Holy fucking shit!

"What the actual fuck are you doing in my apartment? Get out!" Turning to face him, I point to the door, my other hand firmly on my hip.

"We have a date, *Dolcezza*. And you're late." He's leaning against my door frame, arms folded, and I swear he looks like he's about to burst out of the black button-down shirt he's wearing. I'm almost disappointed that he's got the sleeves rolled all the way down again, covering up what I'm guessing are porn-worthy forearms.

Maybe that's for the best though. Temptation and all that.

"We have an appointment. It's not a date. And it's literally one minute past seven. I wouldn't call that late. Now, get the fuck out of my apartment. I'll grab my bag and meet you down there in a couple of minutes." Completely ignoring the fact that he's blocking most of the doorway,

I stride toward him with all the confidence I can muster. I will not be intimidated in my own home.

Not again.

The fucker doesn't move to let me pass, so I stand my ground, toe-to-toe with this giant of a man—even in my six-inch stilettos—and fold my arms across my chest. His eyes dip from my face, but only briefly, and I know he was checking the girls out. I may or may not have pushed them up with my arms on purpose.

His deep gray eyes bore into mine, assessing me for weaknesses. He will find none. I won't back down from this man. He's in my space, we play by my rules. I'm guessing "his guy" is responsible for him being inside my goddamn apartment. Well, he can also go fuck himself right off a fucking cliff.

Seconds later—although it almost felt like hours—he takes a deep breath before moving aside to let me pass.

"Thank you." I'm not a complete bitch, I have manners.

Striding through to my living room, I grab my small black clutch bag from the table. It's already filled with all my essentials—as I said, I was ready to leave before Mr. Asshole gave me a time limit.

He still hasn't left, just continues to glare at me from the doorway, now with a smirk creeping onto his face.

"Are you ready to go, or what?" I rest my hand on my hip and gesture to the door.

His silent stare is almost as annoying as when he speaks. At least I can admire the way his dark hair falls in messy, styled waves across his forehead, the tips close to reaching his eyes.

Without saying a word, he pushes off from the door frame and basically stalks toward me. The move is intimidating, and after what I've been through lately, it should scare me. But it doesn't. As much of an arrogant prick as Marco Mancini is, something inside me says he won't hurt me. He's just a man who's used to getting his own way, and from the little research I've been able to do this afternoon, I've discovered he donates to a women's refuge once a month. Which tells me he's not as big of an asshole as he comes across. There is actually a heart hidden somewhere beneath all those muscles.

I find myself stepping back as he nears me, my back hitting the wall as he cages me in. Keeping my head held high, I give him the same death-glare he's giving me and raise a brow.

"Being on time is very important to me. Our contract will detail that you must be available and on time, *exactly* when I say so. Each time this requirement is not met, you will be punished. Got it?"

"I'm not agreeing to that. We could've left five minutes ago if you'd stop with this entitled alpha crap. You're the one making us late. Does that mean you need a punishment too?"

There's a flicker of amusement in his eyes before he wets his lips, and I have no idea why I find it so fucking sexy.

"Is that appealing to you, River Fox? Punishing me?"

Absolutely it is. But I'm not showing all my cards to this man. This dinner is a one-time thing. I've already decided I'm not taking the job. I'm choosing to ignore his question and concentrate on the fact that he keeps calling me by my fucking name.

"My name is Rose. You will call me Rose."

"No, I will call you by your name. It would be a tragedy to call you anything else." His voice is but a mere growl over my lips, and the scent of vanilla fills my nostrils with him this close. I'd bet my life on the fact that Marco Mancini is anything but vanilla.

"Rose *is* my name." Albeit my middle name, but his *guy* probably told him that already too.

A low laugh escapes his throat before he takes a deep breath. "No."

This man seems determined to push all my buttons, and not the fun ones.

"Are you brave enough to take your first punishment this evening, River Fox? I'll accept my own punishment alongside you. Are you game?"

Now, my first thought is to tell him to fuck all the way off and argue some more about him using my full name. But I'm intrigued, and I rarely back down from a challenge.

"What are the terms?"

His mouth transforms into a predatory grin, mirth dancing in his eyes as he nods once, seemingly impressed with my answer. Stepping back from me, he reaches into his pants pocket. I'd figured he was pleased to see me, but it seems he actually does have a box or something in there.

My eyes widen in surprise as he pulls out a bright pink fucking love-egg-dildo-thing, holding it up for me to get a better look, like I've never seen one before.

"You will wear this to, at, and on the way home from the restaurant." I go to interrupt, but he stops me by placing a hand over my mouth.

Rude.

He removes his hand from my mouth, and I'm in complete shock. I mean, the man wants me to wear a remote-controlled dildo and clit stimulator. I should be kicking him the fuck out of my apartment, but there's something inside of me that wants to do what he's asking. Or telling.

"If I agree to this, then my terms are that you not touch me for the rest of the evening. No skin contact at all. Which means no more covering up my fucking mouth with your paw of a hand."

"Language. I let the first few slide because we're in your space, but, River, don't test me." This time, his growl sends those delicious tingles right between my legs. God-damnit.

"First of all, it's Rose. Second of all, you let it *slide*? Are you kidding me, right now? No man tells me what I can and cannot say. Especially in my free time. Now, we can discuss this at dinner, because frankly, you're making me claustrophobic in my own apartment, and you've outstayed your welcome. Not that you had one in the first place. And lastly, do you agree to the terms or not?"

"Good girl." The look on his face is one of pure hunger, and I realize I didn't swear once during my little rant at him.

"Fucking fuck." Like a child on a playground, I stick my tongue out at him and fold my arms across my chest again, waiting for him to bite at my bratty behavior.

He doesn't.

Instead, he steps forward, and whispers the tips of his fingers from my forehead, down my cheek and to my chin. Not once does he touch me, but he's so close, I can feel the heat coming from every move.

"*Si*, I agree." He hands me the—thankfully sealed—box, and turns to leave. Halfway out, he looks over his shoulder and pierces me with his steel-gray eyes. "Downstairs, two minutes, *Dolcezza*." And then he's gone, closing the door quietly behind him. Who would've thought the big brute could be so gentle?

Marco was silent in the car on the way here, but it wasn't an uncomfortable silence, and the vibrations from the rumbling engine felt pretty damn good. The smirk he had on his face during the fifteen-minute ride remains as we enter the restaurant. He's stayed true to his word so far and hasn't touched me, I'm just wondering when he's planning on activating the love-egg thing I have inside my pussy.

The smartly dressed waiter shows us to a table in the corner by the windows with a great view of the giant Pepsi-Cola sign by the river. I've never actually been here before, and now I'm wondering why, since it's so close to my apartment. The general atmosphere is warm and cozy, but also romantic and classy.

Mental note: Come back here when I'm not with a giant asshole.

Once we arrive at the table, Marco surprises me by moving past the waiter to pull out my chair, gesturing for me to sit. Before he takes his own seat, he leans down and smells my neck. He's so close I can feel the heat coming off him in waves, but he still doesn't physically touch me.

"This is the last time you will wear this wig, *Dolcezza*." The words are whispered into my ear, before he moves to the chair opposite me. It sends a shiver down my spine that I'm trying desperately to suppress, I won't let him see how he's affecting me.

The waiter—who just stood by, awkwardly watching our whole interaction—hands over the wine menu, and before I can decline, Marco does it for me.

"*Due* sparkling waters, *per favore*."

I remain silent, it seems Mr. Mancini has done his homework on me. Drinking with clients or potential clients isn't something I tend to do very often.

Just how much does this guy know about me?

Having already made my mind up that I'm not taking this job, my own research this afternoon was minimal, so I feel at a slight disadvantage for the first time with this man.

"*Sì,* I'll be back with your drinks and to take your food order."

With the waiter gone, I lean forward on my elbows, giving Mr. Asshole a great view of my cleavage.

"What color would you prefer I wear?" Raising my eyebrow in challenge, I twirl a strand of my brown wig around my finger and watch for his reaction.

"None." It's a barely audible snarl, before he picks up his phone and almost sends me shooting off the chair in shock.

I manage to contain my squeal and compose myself. It's over almost as quickly as it started. Fucker's got the app for this love-egg on his phone. It feels like he just turned it up all the way for a few seconds, leaving my clit throbbing for it to continue.

It doesn't.

"Is this how tonight's going to play out? You zap me every time I don't give you what you want?"

His response is a dangerous smile, and another shot of vibrations inside my pussy.

I glare at him. As best I can anyway, I already feel flushed and my nipples are so hard they're poking against the lace of my bra.

Cunt.

The waiter comes back before anything else is said, placing our glasses on the table and taking our orders before nodding and walking away.

I had expected Marco to be a complete asshole and order for me, and I was ready to shut that shit right down. There's no way he could have guessed my order, no matter how much research he had done, and I'm glad he didn't take that choice away from me. I would cut a bitch for messing with my food.

"I'm still confused as to what your punishment this evening is, Mr. Mancini. Care to enlighten me?"

I want to slap the grin that appears off his rugged face, but he'd probably enjoy that.

"My punishment is not laying a finger on you until our contract begins tomorrow."

"How is that a bad thing?"

He lets out a lowly chuckle. "Because, *Dolcezza*, in my world, I take what I want. Restraint isn't one of my virtues. But make no mistake, I will have you screaming my name in ecstasy. Just not tonight."

Cocky cunt. He's so sure of himself, so confident, and everything about his demeanor says he believes he's speaking the absolute truth.

We'll see, asshole.

"Oh!" Fuck, he's playing around with the app for the love-egg again. It's now a low vibration inside my pussy. And holy shit, it feels so good. Not quite orgasm good though... yet. Steeling my spine, because I will not give in to this man, I take a deep breath and put my business head on.

I can totally ignore the toy. I'm a goddamn professional.

"So I think we need to discuss your terms for the offer. I'll be honest, there's not really anything that will sway my decision, but I'm willing to hear you out."

The love-egg changes tempo, causing me to straighten my spine suddenly, and a smirk plays on his lips as he answers. "I need you for three months. For two of those, you will be my wife. And I'm sure you've put a dent in your research and already know exactly who I am. Which means, being my wife comes with rules."

I scoff. He's all about the rules, wife or not.

"Rules which are present for your safety, and mine, *Dolcezza*. I am a powerful man in this city. With power comes danger." He ups the pressure on the love-egg, and the vibrations are running over my clit now too, causing me to adjust in my seat to try and stop it touching my sensitive bud directly.

My curiosity is also piqued now, because, yes, I did do a little research this afternoon, and from what I can gather, Marco Mancini is geared to be the next CEO of Mancini Hotels. His dad is currently the big boss man, but Marco already runs the day-to-day things from what I gather. There were a few articles about the Mancinis' having mafia connections, but I haven't dug deep enough to find out much more. I would hazard a guess that he'll inherit what he's calling 'his' once he's married. His dad comes across as a very traditional man. Well, on the Internet he does anyway.

"Okay. Well, it may seem minimal in the grand scheme of things..." I close my eyes and a low moan escapes my throat before I pin him with my stare. "Will you let me speak? How are we supposed to discuss this if you keep turning up the pressure?"

"Oh, *Dolcezza*. This is your punishment, remember? Allowing me to watch you come undone without a single touch is something I will treasure."

"Don't try sweet-talking me now, asshole."

Oh my fucking gods, I need to stand, to walk, to move! Anything other than sit and take this onslaught of pleasure on my clit.

"Sit down."

I didn't even realize I'd moved. Letting out another moan, and trying to stop it all at once, I sit back down and cross my legs, shuffling forward onto the edge of my chair.

"Marco, turn that thing off." My voice is so deep, my breaths becoming heavy as I try desperately to control what's going on downstairs. "Ohmygod!"

"Do you have terms you wish to discuss with me?" Smug asshole rests his chin on his fist and continues to watch me struggling to contain myself.

Deep breath in through my nose, deep breath out through my mouth. *I've got this.*

Maybe one more deep breath in and out...

"Okay, safe words. Oh... mmm... And we'd need to seriously discuss color and style options... mmm. Shit." I refuse to look around at the semi-busy restaurant, keeping my moans low enough that, to anyone else, I probably just look like I really need to pee. Shuffling around, trying to adjust where the love-egg is hitting so I don't straight up orgasm on this chair, I maintain eye contact with the smug asshole opposite me.

"No wig." He raises a brow and taps a button on his phone, intensifying the feelings inside my pussy and against my clit.

"Yes! To the wig... I always wear..." Another deep breath out through my mouth. "A wig." I'm so close, the pressure is building inside me, and I don't think my deep and concentrated breathing is going to stop it.

"Oh look, the waiter is bringing our dinner, *Dolcezza*." *Tap, tap.*

Oh shit. It's coming... I'm coming.

My moans are escaping of their own accord now, I'm helpless against the sounds coming from my mouth as I try desperately to contain myself.

"*Per favore, cameriere.*"

The waiter's face is full of concern as he places my plate in front me.

"Are you all right, *Signorina*?"

"Mmmhmm. Si. Yep. Fantastic. Yes!" I turn my pending orgasm into some kind of over-enthusiastic compliment, which doesn't remove his confused expression, but he does nod his head and walk away.

"You're an asshole. Oh holy shit." It's happening. And I'm powerless to stop it. I lean back in my seat, stand up, sit back down, stand up again and rest my hands against the table as it hits me. The tingling from my clit spreads throughout my body, and I squeeze my lids closed to breathe through it, keeping my voice as quiet as possible.

"Eyes on me, *Dolcezza*."

Argh, this man! Defiantly, I open my eyes and glare at him as the aftershocks continue until I'm finally able to sit down again. The love-egg has stopped vibrating now, and Marco's eyes are on mine, the steel-gray almost black with an animalistic desire.

"Did you enjoy that, asshole?"

"Very much so, but the evening has only just begun, River Fox."

CHAPTER FOUR
RIVER

Marco's car drops me off just after nine-thirty and instead of going on his merry way, the driver waits for me to walk up the stoop, say hello to my favorite human, and pretend that I'm walking inside. I watch as he slowly pulls out of his space along the sidewalk before I walk right back outside and plop down next to Mr. Bobby.

"It's nice to see some men are still gentlemanly." He points his chin to the place where the car was sitting only moments ago.

"Nah, it's his driver, so he's paid to make sure I walk right in and am safe from the dangers of the big, bad, city. Pfft." Pulling one shoe off, I rub my aching toes as my head falls on Mr. Bobby's shoulder.

"Everything all right, sweet girl?" He pats my hand as he brings his cup of tea to his mouth and takes a dainty sip.

"Yeah, I just... I don't know. Adulting is hard and I have decisions to make. So many decisions." I repeat my toe-massaging ritual with my other foot and enjoy the rare moment of complete and utter silence.

"Try me." Looking up at Mr. Bobby, I'm certain my confusion is written all over my face because he quickly elaborates. "Tell me about your decisions and I'll tell you what I think. I'm old and therefore wise." He chuckles like he's making a joke, but I do believe he's the wisest of all New Yorkers, and he's my friend. The angel that sits on the opposite shoulder from my devil. A devil that suspiciously looks more and more like Marco Mancini.

"Well, I don't want to shock you. My life isn't exactly pure and angelic." A smile forms at the corners of my lips, imagining how outraged Mr. Bobby would be if he knew what I do for a living.

"Sweet, sweet, child. I have seen too many things in this lifetime to be shocked about any of it. There's absolutely nothing you can say that would change my opinion of you." I can hear him taking another sip and for a moment I consider that maybe... just maybe... I could confide in him.

"Centuries of societal norms say otherwise." Pretty much sums it all up.

"All right, then. Let's pretend I don't know that you're not a... what's that you call it? A life coach?" My eyes were beginning to droop from the sheer fatigue of my last two days. Or two months. Hell, maybe I'm just exhausted from the last eight years. But his comment gives me a shot of adrenaline throughout my entire body. Lifting my head from his shoulder, I look up at him and try to read his features. He's completely stoic, his eyes staring straight ahead, his mouth an unwavering line. Until, that is, he turns slightly in my direction and raises a brow.

Holy fuck. Does he really know? I want to hide in the darkest, deepest hole of the city and pretend this conversation is not happening.

"But..." Speechless. That's what I am.

"Let's just say you've got a lot of rich boyfriends for someone living in a building where the best security option is an old man with a curious mind." *Just kill me now.* "So, now that the cat's out of the bag, tell me what's going on."

"I'm going to need more than just a cup of tea to get this conversation on the way." I'm about to stand when Mr. Bobby reaches behind him and hands me a bottle of Johnnie Walker.

"Well, well, well. It seems I'm not the only one with secrets around here. And all this time, I thought you were drinking tea to help you sleep." We both chuckle as he hands me a clean cup.

"Who says I don't? That whisky is my guarantee that I'll sleep like a baby. Now quit dilly dallying and let's figure out your life plan." Fuck, I love this man.

"Mr. Bobby? Will you marry me?" His entire body shakes as his deep, throaty laugh erupts from his chest.

"Ah, sweet child. In many ways, I already have. You are so much like Josie, you could have been our daughter." My heart constricts, those words a balm to my very soul.

"I can't think of a better compliment."

"Only the truth, River. Only the truth. Now, what are our options here?"

I tell him about Kai. About our complicated relationship and about his announcement to marry Freya.

"Well, if this was the Bachelorette, I'd say he'd be eliminated in the first round." I think he's joking but the growl gives him away. He's not on Team Kai, apparently.

"It's complicated, Mr. Bobby. I don't think he's doing it because he wants to, you know. Like, I think there's something more to it but I don't know what it is." It was too soon and too fast. Kai isn't normally such a hot head.

"River, if there's anything you take away from our conversations, let it be this..." Placing his tea on the step above us, he turns fully to look me in the eyes. "Life is only as complicated as you decide to make it. The sooner you realize that you are the main character in your story, the clearer your decision-making will be." We stare at each other as I digest his words.

"But feelings aren't simple. I love Kai. I always have. But Nathaniel... he's everything I've ever wanted in a man. Kind and caring. Attentive." Mr. Bobby nods, a sound of approval coming from his direction tells me he's definitely on Team Candy-Aisle-Guy.

"He's a doctor, being kind, caring, and attentive is a big part of his job so it makes sense that you'd be attracted to that part of him. Sounds to me that the decision is more than simple, it's evident." I laugh because I haven't told him about Marco Mancini yet and that's going to blow any episode of the Bachelorette right out of the water.

"Well, tonight, I have a client who's offering me a way out of this, but it's a contract that could mean the end to Nathaniel being an option."

"All right, now. Give me the details."

I go through the entire conversation at the coffee shop and then at dinner. As I talk, I feel myself getting animated and aggravated at every little control tactic Marco played. Obviously, I left out the part where he made me come in the very public restaurant with a very active egg in my fucking vagina. By the time I'm finished going over this entire shit show, I'm standing, my arms flailing all around as I finish off my story with him putting me in a private car and tapping the roof as a sign for the driver to take off.

"Can you believe the nerve of that guy? There's no way I can survive three months of his crap. I'll end up killing him." By the time I'm finished with my diatribe, I'm exhausted all over again, slumping against the railing and taking a much needed shot of Johnnie Walker.

"Interesting."

"That's it? I tell you I'm in a messy bind and that's your wise word of the night?" *Hmph*, that was a waste of time.

"What's interesting is how passionate you are when talking about this man who clearly makes your blood boil." Why does he have a smirk on his face? Is he…?

"Are you mocking me, Mr. Bobby?" With my fists on my hips, I stare down at him, giving him my best annoyed face.

"Well, I'm amused but no, I'm not making fun of you. Ain't my style, sweet girl. Now, come sit."

With a big sigh, I'm back at Mr. Bobby's side, my elbows resting on the step behind me.

"Sounds to me like you're missing the big picture."

"And what picture is that?" Looking at my toes, I realize I need to go back to the salon for a pedicure.

"Right now, Kai isn't in the picture. It don't matter why he's getting married, what matters is that he *is* getting married. As far as Nathaniel is concerned, I say the truth is the only way to go. If he really wants you for you, then he'll be part of the conversation. But, River, let me tell you something. Ain't no man gonna want his girl to be married to another. No amount of money is worth that sacrifice."

"Yeah, I know." The silence grows until he gives me his next words and I almost choke on my saliva.

"That said, I've never seen you so riled up as when you talk about this Marco fella. Josie always said that she knew I was the one because I infuriated and made her horny all at the same time."

I have no idea what he's talking about.

"Good morning, Mr. Bobby!"

"Sweet girl, why are you up so early?" I bend at the waist and kiss my favorite neighbor on the crown of his balding head.

"Early bird and all that. I've got a business meeting. How's that 'youngster' coffee treating you?" Last week, I introduced the deliciousness that is hazelnut mocha to Mr.

Bobby as a token of my appreciation for him. He'd scoffed, telling me he only drinks coffee the way God meant for it to be: black—occasionally with a drop of whisky.

"It's gonna be the death of me. For real, all this sugar is gonna kill me." I shrug at his words.

"Nah, you're stronger than sugar. You're invincible!"

"Go on, go grab your own deadly concoction or else your business meeting will be a bust." Blowing him a sassy little kiss, I skip down the stairs and speed walk to my favorite coffee shop before heading to Polly's office.

So far, her company is running smoothly. Her secretary is a mastermind and her girls have enough autonomy that my job replacing Polly is actually pretty easy.

My only hiccup is Frank constantly calling me to keep me updated on this or that.

Sally hasn't worked in two days.

Brandy is getting too involved with one of her johns.

Lucie has gained a couple of pounds. That one I responded to with an angry emoji and a middle finger telling him her weight was none of his fucking business.

He apologized. Profusely.

I walk the whole way up to Midtown and across to the West Side. I could have taken the subway, but early mornings mean lots of people and honestly, too many of them forget that showers exist.

Not to mention that I have my power suit on with my heels securely placed in my backpack.

"Good morning, Ms. Fox."

"Good morning, Sheryl."

"I have all of the schedules here for the week. Lina is out sick until next Tuesday, we're compensating her as per the contract. Frank has notified me that Brandy may be having a personal relationship with her client, let me see..." She flicks through her pages while I read the updates, noticing that Brandy does, in fact, spend a lot of time with Mr. Beckett.

"Yes, Mr. Beckett. He's a Senator. I think his re-election campaign starts soon." Reading the man's bio and all the background checks Polly had done on him, I stumble on a name that makes my skin tingle.

Eleonor Hunter is his biggest contributor.

Why does that name sound familiar? I'm about to ask Sheryl about this when Frank walks in and practically grunts his hello.

"Rose, looking beautiful as always." I smile, nod, and just as I'm about to ask about Eleonor, Frank interrupts me again.

"We should talk." His voice is grave, his normally neutral facial expression has a slight worry to it, which means it has to be important.

"Thank you, Sheryl, for this. Remind me to ask you about some of the names on here. I'll meet with Frank and then call you in."

"Sure thing. I'll get to work on sending appointment reminders to our clients. Just buzz me in when you're ready." I'm guessing the confused look on my face is what prompts her to elaborate. "The phone? Just press the yellow button and I'll know you're ready for me."

I smile gratefully at her, knowing she's pretty much the backbone of this company and is the only reason I'm not running Polly's business into the ground.

"Okay, Frank, let's do this."

Both inside Polly's office, I close the door and sit behind her desk. I've often seen my clients—big business men or powerful politicians—using their desks as a tool to their advantage. I feel it now. The desk is a wide berth. A separation between them and you. It's a way to establish hierarchy.

"What's going on, Frank?"

He doesn't sit. Instead, he wears a path on the carpeted floor as he paces from one side to the other.

"Hey, sit. You're making me dizzy with your stress walking." Frank turns to me, his crooked nose more visible from his standing position and my sitting one. He's a big guy, a mixture of muscle and too many donuts.

"All right, Rose, I'm just going to say it outright." I reel in the urge to roll my eyes at his overly dramatic display of urgency. Just spit it out, dude.

"I feel like there's a connection. A very deep one." He stops pacing, his hands on his wide hips and his black eyes staring intently at me. His Brooklyn accent is even more prominent than usual.

"A connection? You mean Brandy and the politician? Don't worry about it, I'll call her in today and have a chat with her." Crossing one leg over the other, I lean my elbows on the desk and notice he's still wound up.

"No, not Brandy. That's not what—"

"There's another girl getting personally involved with a client? Shit, feelings are spreading like a virus around here." It's meant to be a joke, a way to calm him down. I didn't realize he was so invested in this business. That said, he's been with Polly for so long, I'm guessing when work runs smoothly, so does his life.

"No, it's not like that." He's getting agitated and it's making me impatient.

"Just say it, Frank. I've got a lot on my plate today."

"Yeah, I fuckin' noticed." Every hair on my body stands upright at the tone of his voice.

"Excuse me?" I'm now on high alert, my muscles tense and ready for a fight.

"Sorry, sorry. I'm just... okay. I'll just say it."

"Fucking finally." I murmur low enough that I hope he doesn't hear me.

"Will you have dinner with me tonight?" There's a beat—more like several—where the entire office, the building, maybe the whole of New York City, goes completely silent. I know we're both breathing since no one is choking, but I can't for the life of me hear it or feel it.

A million questions run through my brain, starting with his loyalty to Polly and ending with his age that's closer to my parents' than mine.

Not to mention that I'm just not attracted to him on any level. But as a woman, I am constantly aware of the dynamics between myself and any man in the room. His physical strength, his emotional state, his threat level.

Right now, I'm on high alert because Frank's obvious stress is not reassuring me.

"Erm, I'm incredibly flattered." By flattered, I mean freaked out. "And any girl would be honored to be your date, but I don't think that's a great idea." What I want to say is, *"Sorry, bud, but I'm just not into you like that."* Except, I have no idea how he would react to the truth. My only option is to stroke his ego a little so he doesn't expect me to stroke anything else of his.

"Why wouldn't it be?" He's now standing a little taller, which means I need to be very careful with how I answer him. Egos are a tricky thing in the male species.

"Because we work together. It's never good to mix business and pleasure." I grace him with what I'm hoping is a placating smile.

"Right but you're only here for a little while. It's not like you're an actual employee." *Fuck.*

"Look, Frank. You're a great guy but I'm not in a place in my life that allows me to be dating seriously." I mean, it's definitely the truth. Nathaniel is giving me the space I need to decide what I really want in my life. Nathaniel is perfect. He's caring and attentive, but I'm afraid he's lost hope for us. Or maybe he's just giving me the space he thinks I need. In fact, I haven't even seen him at the grocery store. I made it a point to go at his usual times but I still haven't "run into" him.

Maybe he's truly done with me.

As I map out all of the different scenarios, the only thing I'm truly certain about is that I'd like to change paths. I'd like to actually have a job that I can brag about. Something legit. Something that makes a difference. Most of all, I'd like to share that part of my world with the man I love.

All I need to figure out now is, who exactly do I love? Who do I want by my side for the rest of my life?

"That's bullshit and you know it." There goes that temper of his again, his accent coming back in force.

"To be honest, that attitude is exactly the reason I'm not keen on having dinner or lunch or fucking breakfast with you. Is *that* clear?"

Deflating just a little bit, Frank's shoulders hunch and his brows furrow like he's trying to figure out the mathematical formula for the theory of relativity.

"But you have time for Nathaniel Reed?"

For the second time this morning, my shoulders tense and the hairs on my skin stand straight up.

"How the fuck do you know about Nathaniel?" It's my turn to feel anger. It seems like all the fucking men around me are privy to my personal life and it's getting out of fucking control.

"Polly had me do a background check on him. From there, I found out about your little trip to Niagara Falls.

Had time for that, didn't ya?" He takes a step closer, his beefy palms pressed hard against the wooden surface of Polly's desk.

Does he think he can intimidate me so easily?

I stand, my heels making me feel more powerful than I truly am.

"What I do in my private or professional life has absolutely nothing to do with you, Frank. So, unless you want me to tell Polly you've been basically stalking me, I suggest you walk the fuck away right now." I have no idea how my voice is staying so calm and even, because inside, I'm shaking like a fucking leaf. Frank's sheer size could squash me in a matter of seconds. But I am no man's bitch and least of all someone who's violating my privacy.

We have a stare off for what feels like a century before he growls and walks out of the office. It's only when he's gone that I can feel my hands and knees shake from the exchange.

Giving myself a couple of minutes to calm down, I look at the phone sitting on the desk and debate whether I call Sheryl in or get Polly on the phone to demand some fucking answers.

Buzzing in Sheryl, I have her come in and go over the week's schedule, preparing and adjusting for the clients, but also making sure our new girls have a clean bill of health as well as birth control. It's what I respect the most about Polly. She may be ruthless, but she created her empire from a shabby studio with less-than-respectable johns. Today, her priority is the well-being of her girls.

"Okay, so a girl called Lou-Lou called about a dancer position, shall we wait until Polly's back or can you deal with that?"

"Schedule her in for an interview, I'll take care of it."

"Oh, by the way, the new girl Sabrina?"

"Yeah, the blond pixie?" I remember her because girls with short hair in our business are a rarity.

"Yes. Her file says she'll gladly take on male or female clients so we've scheduled the Mayor's daughter who has particular kinks." Ah, those are the clients who pay the most to keep their secrets hidden away.

"Good. It's like we're serving our country." We both laugh at my ridiculous joke when the landline rings. Sheryl picks up and answers "Polly's Events and Planning. Hi, Polly! Yeah, she's right here. I'll pass you over. Have fun wherever you are!" I smile at Sheryl's enthusiasm. We're all so happy our boss lady is having a good time. It's well deserved.

We have some small talk for a while as Sheryl gets her things and gives us privacy. It's when I realize there's a break in our conversation that I ask what I've been needing to know.

"So, I got a job offer yesterday." My voice is tentative because I'm almost certain of what she's going to say.

"Must be interesting if you're running it by me." Ever the perceptive one.

"Well, he's a powerful man needing to secure a powerful position." I think about everything Marco told me last night, then my mind focuses on the egg in my pussy and I have to squeeze my things together to assuage the need that comes over me instantly.

"Aren't they all?" I'd told him as much, but this was different, wasn't it?

"Three months, *married*." I put the emphasis on the last word to make sure she gets my dilemma.

"How much?" Her voice is all business now, and it's exactly what I need. Not a romantic Mr. Bobby telling me I'm all "riled up" for Marco Mancini. He has no idea what he's talking about.

"Two mil now, three in three months."

Silence.

The only reason I know she's still on the line is because I can hear her breathing. So, I wait as she processes. Polly's thinking about all the angles. I've learned to read her, so I give her the time she needs to gift me with her wisdom.

"It's your ticket out, River. If that's what you want. Five million dollars can do a lot of good in your world. You could even buy me out and run your own company." *What now?*

"Buy you out? Are you considering retiring?"

"Maybe, but I refuse to sell to just anyone. I won't retire until I know whoever is buying will have my girls' best interest in mind." I get a little bubble of excitement buzzing in my gut at her words. This news could be a game changer. "You're my girl, Rose. I know you'd make sure my business stays clean and respectable."

"Yeah, you know I would." My words are whispered as my mind reels from this information.

"Take the gig, save your money. And if you decide you want to buy me out, I'll sell in a heartbeat."

What did Mr. Bobby say last night?

Big picture. I must look at the big picture.

Chapter Five

River

Both Polly and Mr. Bobby have really made me think about my life choices. I mean, my brother's a big boy now, all grown up and married. Apart from some student loans and a small mortgage—that I pay—he has his own home, a growing business, everything he could possibly need to live a successful and happy life.

So why am I still using him as an excuse to live the way I am?

If I'm honest with myself, I've been miserable for a while, telling myself I'm doing this for Ev, for his happiness because he's my responsibility. But he's not—not anymore—and I'm sure if he knew what has been going on, he wouldn't want this for me either.

I love him with all my heart and soul, and I don't think he relies on me as heavily as I've convinced myself he does.

Don't get me wrong, I'm not ashamed of what I do, I'm just… tired. Tired of pretending, tired of the lies, tired of never getting my own happily ever after.

"Hey there, sweet girl. You look like you have the weight of the world on your shoulders. Come and have some tea and tell me about your meeting." He grabs his thermos and a spare cup that he always keeps on hand and pours me a drink. I swear he keeps that extra cup close by for moments like this.

It's only midday, but after spending the morning at Polly's place, a little afternoon drink isn't the worst idea. I don't exactly have plans for the rest of the afternoon thanks to Marco's *guy* interfering with my appointments. *Fucker*.

"Thank you, Mr. Bobby." Smiling, I approach the stoop and bend down for a much-needed hug. He gives the best hugs. They're always short and sweet, but the aura around this man is calming and powerful all at once. He gives a tight squeeze and lets go before handing me my cup.

I sit just as a car horn and less-than-polite language wafts through the chilly December air.

"Aren't you cold?" I know I said Mr. Bobby was invincible but it was just a figure of speech. I'd hate for him to get sick out here.

"I've got my coat, what little is left on my head is covered." Glancing at his Giants knit beanie, I scoff.

"I was hoping you'd be a Jets fan. I guess nobody's perfect, huh? Not even you, Mr. Bobby." He chuckles at that and takes a sip of his heavily dosed tea *à la* whisky. I suppose that's keeping him warm, too. Good thing it's sunny out today.

"Ah, looky there. Little Serena Lopez had her baby." Just as he finishes his phrase, aforementioned Serena waves in his direction shouting that she'll come by in a minute to introduce him to the newborn.

For the first time in my life, I allow myself to wonder if I could be like Serena one day. Walking along the streets of New York City with a baby tucked into his stroller and growing up with the sounds of life all around.

The honking, the yelling, the music drifting from the open window in the Spring. The chatter on the sidewalks as neighbors run into each other. The tourists asking for directions when their phone GPS leads them astray. Sure, we'll answer like we're too busy for their afternoon strolls, but deep inside, we're proud to know The City inside and out.

"That young woman has come a long way, you know. Her mother raised all four kids with love and strict rules.

I told her that deadbeat husband of hers was gonna be a handful." I have no idea who these people are, but listening to Mr. Bobby is like having a grandpa who relays stories from generation to generation.

"You know, if I ever have kids, I'm going to need you to dole out some good wisdom so I don't screw them up." With a sigh, I swallow what's left of my tea—mostly whisky—and place the cup on the tray.

"Well, I have to go upstairs. I haven't talked to my brother in a while and he gets worried. Then he calls a bazillion times and annoys me."

Laughing, he nods his head like it all makes perfect sense.

Before I reach the door, I turn back around and wrap my arms around Mr. Bobby, whispering a heartfelt thank you for always making me feel better.

"See you tom—"

"River! Move!"

"Wha—"

Before I can even get my words out, Mr. Bobby seems to find the strength of ten men and pushes me roughly away from him, his hot drink scalding my hand. It's so out of character, I barely have time to think. The force of his push is so strong, I can't stay on my feet, and I fall to the ground, hard. My head hits the step and pain shoots through my brain just before everything goes black.

The sound of screeching tires and people shouting brings me back and I open my eyes, still with the throbbing pain in my head. As my focus comes back, I see Mr. Bobby staring at me. His head level with mine, on the floor. His eyes are full of so much worry, and I don't question why he pushed me, instead I sit up slowly and put a hand to where the pain is coming from. Luckily, my hand comes away with no blood anywhere.

Thank fuck.

I take a deep breath to speak, and turn to Mr. Bobby. Then I see it, the blood underneath him. The hole in his chest.

No...

"Mr. Bobby?" My words are barely audible, merely a whisper.

He smiles at me from where he lies, his eyes watering as he moves his mouth, trying to speak, his warm breath visible in the chilly December air.

"No, don't talk. It's going to be fine. It's fine. I'll call an ambulance and they'll come and they'll save you and everything will be just... *fine.*" I scooch behind him, cradling him between my knees and resting his head on my thigh—making sure his beanie is firmly in place—before I slam my other hand over his wound to keep him from bleeding out.

"Somebody, help!" My screams don't feel loud enough. "Come on, Mr. Bobby, keep your eyes open... Help!"

He continues to look at me, still trying to speak, as I try desperately to keep my calm and grab my phone from my pocket to call an ambulance and the fucking police, and whoever else I need to call to save this sweet man in my arms.

"Don't for-forget the big picture... sweet girl."

"Mr. Bobby. Come on. Eyes open. Help us!"

I can't look away, but at the same time, seeing the despondence in his eyes is heartbreaking, it's almost like his soul is disappearing right in front of me. Well, I won't have that. *No. Not happening.*

"Mr. Bobby, you're just going to have to remind me, aren't you? Every day. You hear me? Don't you dare give up. I need you." I'm trying so hard to hold back my frightened tears, but it's not working. They're streaming down my face and onto his head, where I attempt to wipe them away.

"Josie?" His voice is so quiet I can barely hear him, and he's not looking at me anymore. His eyes are half closed, and the serene smile on his face causes a sob to tear from my throat.

I dial 911 on my cell, turn on the speakerphone, and put it on the step next to me.

Why the fuck is nobody around? Where are all the people? I know this street can be quiet sometimes, but why the fuck now?

"Nine-one-one, what's your emergency?" Comes through the speaker.

"My friend has been shot, please come quickly." I reel off the address, and before I can hang up or do anything else, Mr. Bobby slowly moves his hand over mine on his chest, bringing all my attention back to him. The woman on the other end of the line says something about the police and ambulance being on their way, which means someone else already called it in.

He pats my hand twice before it slips to his side.

"Jo..." His voice is just a breath, spoken on an exhale.

"It's okay, Mr. B. The ambulance is on the way."

Something's wrong though. His chest no longer rises and falls beneath my hand, the low, shallow breaths he was taking before have stopped, and the whole world begins to crumble around me.

No...

I can feel myself screaming at him to wake up, ordering him to breathe and open his eyes. I can barely see through the tears streaming down my cheeks.

"Wake up. I *need* you. Please, Mr. Bobby. Wake up."

The sirens blare in the distance, but they're too late. He's gone, and I feel so broken inside. I have no idea what happened, but I know he pushed me for a reason.

He saved me.

Mr. Bobby saved my life, and paid with his own.

The agony inside me is roaring, and I know my screams for help were heard by the crowd of people around us. But it's too much. I don't want them to touch him, to hurt him. To take him away from me where I'll never see him again.

An ambulance pulls up, moving the onlookers away to get to us. I can barely make them out through my blurred vision, but one of them is crouched down and speaking to me, trying to gently pry my arms from around Mr. Bobby.

I let out an almighty yell of frustration, anger, and heartache before finally releasing him. The ding of my stupid phone makes me pick it up, about to throw it in frustration, but the message I see flashing there makes me pause.

Unknown: That was supposed to be for you.

The throbbing in my head comes back tenfold, and a darkness appears in the corner of my vision. My arms feel heavy and I hear someone next to me speaking, asking for my name, before I fall into nothingness.

Chapter Six

River

The scent of sandalwood tickles my nose as I slowly wake up. I don't remember going to bed last night but it must have been late because I'm still tired as fuck. I try to raise my hand to scratch my nose but it's being weighed down by something. Am I lying on my arm?

Sandalwood. Fuck.

I'm afraid to open my eyes, afraid I'll find Kai lying next to me. I'm not that girl. I'm not Freya. Frowning, I try to recall what happened. Mostly, I want to rule out sex with my engaged best friend.

"Kai?" My voice sounds weird. It actually croaked like something was stuck in it. Why can't I move my hand? My nose is itching so bad.

"Thank fuck, River." Kai's voice sounds like it's in a tunnel, a little far away with a slight echo. That's weird. Even stranger is the beeping sound that is slowly getting louder and going faster. Maybe the garbage trucks in my street are backing up.

"What are you doing here?" Fucking hell, I'm so thirsty.

"Can you open your eyes, River?" Blinking once, twice, my lids feel so heavy, I'm almost convinced I got way too high last night and apparently made some really bad decisions.

"How long has she been awake?"

"Since now. Like thirty seconds."

"Ms. Fox? Can you open your eyes?"

I'm trying, you fuckers, just give me a second.

Slowly, my lids lift and the blurry image of two faces staring at me comes into focus. I recognize Kai right away, the woman next to him, not so much.

"There she is." I feel Kai squeezing my hand, his smile as bright as the overhead lights.

"Am I in the hospital?"

And that's when it all comes rushing back to me like a movie reel on fast-forward.

The day at Polly's office.

The tea on the stoop.

The sudden push from Mr. B.

Mr. Bobby.

Oh my God. The blood.

All around me, the beeping noise starts to accelerate to the same rhythm as the beats of my heart.

The blood. So much blood.

"Is Mr. Bobby here? I need to see him. Please." As I push myself off the bed, my head starts to swim from the sudden effort.

"Hey, hey. You need to lie down. Just calm down, okay, Riv?"

I know he's trying to be helpful but right now, I want to punch Kai for being in my way.

"Kai, please. I need to know that he's okay." I almost miss it, the look Kai gives the nurse. It's quick and significant but it's not meant for me. What he doesn't understand is that until I see Mr. Bobby is fine, I won't be able to rest. I won't be able to do anything.

"Look, you have a concussion, River. You passed out in the middle of the street and slept for like three hours. Just... wait a minute, okay?" As he bends down to kiss my forehead, I take advantage of his proximity and curl my fingers around his shirt just below the neckline. Pulling him close to my face, I snarl at him like a feral fucking cat.

"Tell me about Mr. Bobby. Now." It's the sound of his reluctant sigh that breaks me. The first tears blur my vision and just as they fall down my cheeks, he whispers the words I hoped I'd never have to hear.

"He didn't make it, Riv. They did everything they could but he was already gone by the time the ambulance arrived." The hand holding his shirt falls back to the mattress but he picks it up and holds it to his mouth, whispering he's sorry over and over again. His face disappears behind the veil of my blurred vision as I digest the news.

Turning to my side, I curl into the fetal position and cry.

Mr. Bobby is gone and a piece of my heart has just disintegrated.

Once I calm down enough to be coherent, I video chat with Petal and Everest—thanks to Kai's phone—before the police arrive to interview me.

They're worried, of course. It's not every day that I'm in the hospital after being involved in a shooting in broad fucking daylight. Jesus fucking Christ. Who would do that? Why? What the fuck did Mr. Bobby ever do to anyone?

By this time, my memory seems to be back to full capacity but unfortunately, I have no new information to give the police. My back was to the shooter, then I hit my head against the cement. Lights out.

They've interviewed the neighbors and passers-by to get any eye-witness reports, but I don't know much about what they've found.

With no living relatives, the police don't necessarily have to keep me up to date, but I've begged them to do so for my own sanity.

Just as they're walking out with a promise to contact me if they have anything new, I call out to them.

"Officers?"

"Yes, ma'am?" The taller of the two, Officer Lanksy, I think, turns around and looks back at me.

"Did anyone see the car rush off? I think I heard tires screeching when I came to. I mean, I guess it could be a million other cars in New York but... I thought I'd tell you, just in case." There's no way that information can help anyone but I can't help feeling like I'm missing something. Something important.

"Yes, someone did. It was a late model..." he reaches down to look at his notes when his partner pipes up.

"Toyota Corolla, dark. Maybe blue or dark gray." I stare at the younger officer. The two men are opposites in every way. It's obvious Lansky is well into his career while the other is starting. The gray hairs, the laugh lines, the permanent exhaustion in his eyes all tell the story of a man whose job is wearing him down.

"Okay, thank you."

Kai sits on the bed, his thumb rubbing slow circles on the back of my hand, but I can barely feel him. I know he's trying to calm or maybe reassure me, but there's a niggling feeling in the back of my head about this whole situation. Something I can't quite place. A memory that's dancing at the edge of my consciousness that I can't quite grasp.

"How are you feeling? Do you need anything?" Looking back at Kai, I frown. I don't know why it's only just occurred to me, but I can't help voicing my surprise.

"Better, thank you. How did you get here so fast?" I slide my hand out of his and reach for the water sitting on the table beside me, gulping down a healthy dose. The doctors said they were coming by soon to check on me and if my scans look good, I'll be free to go in the morning.

"They called Ev, he's your next of kin. Petal immediately called me and well, I dropped everything to be here as quickly as possible." He shrugs and looks out the window, a shadow settling in his eyes.

"Are *you* okay?" He scoffs like my question is completely ridiculous. The thing is, we're close, he and I. No matter what is happening in our respective lives, Kai will always be my first love. The boy I looked up to practically my entire life. No amount of strange circumstances can take that away from us.

"I'm not the one who... fuck, River. We almost lost you." I see his jaw tighten, a tick forming as he grinds his molars, no doubt trying to control his emotions.

"Hey, I'm here. I'm okay. Close call, but it's all good."

"Stop doing that, River. Don't make it out to be nothing. You should be home with us. Where you're safe." I'm about to answer when the door opens and a tall figure fills the entire entrance.

He's impossible to miss, with a face made for painters. Hair dark as midnight and shoulders strong enough to carry the weight of the world. His eyes pierce right through my soul as he makes his way to my bed with control written in every one of his steps.

He's beautiful, there's no denying it. His power, a gift from the gods. I wish I could say the same about his attitude.

"She'd be bored out of her mind." Then he opens his mouth, and there's the asshole we all know and hate.

"Marco, what the fuck are you doing here?"

"Who the fuck are you?"

Kai and I speak at the same time, earning us an amused tilt of Marco's lips. That's when I see the long-stemmed red rose that he's been hiding behind his back as he holds it out to me and bows like I'm nobility.

"I know a guy." *Of fucking course he does.* "It's ten minutes short of twenty-four hours."

Warily, I take the rose, closing my eyes as I inhale the sweet scent. A heavy weight bumps my finger, surprising me. Looking down at the stem, I gasp when I notice the white gold, princess-cut diamond engagement ring sitting there like a dompter of thorns.

"What the f—"

"*Dolcezza*, what did I say about that language?" Snapping my mouth shut, not because I want to spare him my lashing out, but to avoid doing it in front of Kai—who's looking between us like he can't understand a single word we're saying.

"Ten minutes." Marco whispers as he takes the opposite hand from the one Kai was holding earlier and caresses my ring finger with his thumb. Then, he turns to Kai and, with a growl that hardly seems justified, addresses his comment from before he walked inside the room.

"River doesn't need protecting. She's not a victim, she's a fighter." His gaze lands on me again, and all I see is awe until he turns right back to Kai. "A queen ruling side by side with her king."

Kai turns to me, confused. Pointing a thumb in Marco's direction he asks, "Who the fuck is this guy? A wannabe Good Fella?" I don't miss the sneer from Marco, but I don't address it either. In that ultimate moment, I make a decision.

I look at the big picture.

I think about my future, my investments, my ambitions.

In that moment, I think about myself. Not Kai, not my brother. Not even Nathaniel.

Right then, without a trace of doubt in my voice, I decide.

"He's my fiancé."

CHAPTER SEVEN
RIVER

I t goes without saying, Kai wasn't happy about my decision. Hell, I'm not even sure I'm completely happy with it, but I could have fucking died—if it hadn't been for my own personal guardian angel, Mr. Bobby. I'm allowed to be selfish and think of my own happiness for once.

Petal's always talking about how the universe works in mysterious ways, how it will give people signs and lessons to lead them to their best lives. But sometimes they aren't always what you'd expect, they can come in the form of great happiness or great tragedy. Those are often the moments when decisions need to be made, whether they be large or small, and they can affect so much more than you'd ever imagine.

I'm guessing that's what Mr. Bobby meant by telling me to look at the bigger picture. And though it guts me inside to even think of him not being here, I won't let his sacrifice be wasted.

Freya actually turned up about five minutes ago and practically dragged Kai out of my hospital room before he had the chance to bitch about my announcement. Although, not before her sour face turned to all the false niceties when she spotted Marco in here too.

I get why she doesn't trust Kai alone with me, I'm not stupid, but she needs to tone it down a few gazillion notches because all the red flags are flying over there.

Marco followed them out, tapping at his sparkling gold wristwatch on the way, like the asshole he is. So now, I'm on my own again, in a bright white hospital room, on the most uncomfortable bed in the world, wearing the most hideous hospital gown I could have ever imagined. Bare back and all.

But all those things aren't what's bothering me. I allow a tear to fall from my watery eyes as I remember Mr. Bobby. The serene smile on his face when he whispered his wife's name. The kindness and love in his eyes, even as they were dimming. And even the small squeeze of my hand before I—

Wait a minute. The text message. I remember reading a text on my phone. It has the answer, I'm sure of it. *What did it say?*

"Where's my phone?" I'm talking to myself, but I don't care. I can't recall what the message said, I just know it was important somehow. My movements are stiff, my body achy all over, but it could be worse. I probably need a good stretch and I'll be fine. Sitting all the way up, I look to the bedside table, holding half a glass of water and my rose. No phone.

The ring on my left hand still feels heavy on my finger, and I can't help but love the way it sparkles in the light when I move around. Maybe I'll wear it on a different finger when this is all over. After all, Marco did say I could keep everything he bought for me as part of the contract.

Anyway, phone. Sliding out of bed, I pull off the wires stuck to my body and bend down to look in the cupboard. Nope. Not in there either.

"What a good little wife you'll make. You've got that position nailed, *Dolcezza*."

"What the fuck, Marco?" Spinning around, my heart is racing in my chest and my eyes are wide.

"I'm going to put my dick into that sassy little mouth of yours right here and now if you curse again." He doesn't move from the door and his arms are folded across his chest, making his muscles look like they're trying to escape through the seams of the black button-down shirt he's wearing.

"You wouldn't dare." I narrow my eyes at the cocky bastard, mirroring his stance in defiance.

"Try me." He raises a brow, challenging me, and I really want to see if he's true to his word. Although, I get the feeling he is, and if I didn't have something important to do, like find my fucking phone so I can see that goddamn text message, then I'd be testing my own theory.

Not today, Satan. Not to-fucking-day.

Our stare-off feels like it lasts a lifetime before he speaks again.

"Looking for something?"

I huff and move my hands to my hips. "And the award for observation goes to Marco Mancini."

With a couple of confident strides toward me, his hands sliding into the pockets of his slacks, we're now toe-to-toe. His size and height should intimidate me. Instead, I smirk up at him, loving that I'm getting under his skin. He brings a hand up to my face, fingers around my jaw with his palm on my neck, and leans down so his stormy gray eyes are level with mine.

I'm sure he's about to give me a telling off, and before I can voice my defense, his lips are on mine. It's not soft, and the low growl he emits as his tongue demands entrance has my nipples hardening against the scratchy hospital gown. I bring my hands up to his chest to push him away, but he grabs my wrists with his free hand and holds them there, pinning me to his solid body.

When he pulls away, sucking my tongue as he goes, he lets me go and I stumble. His arms shoot out to steady me, and he grabs my hips to sit me back onto the bed.

"Stay. Now, what are you looking for?"

My lips feel swollen, but I won't let him see he's affecting me. Instead, I let out another small huff and mumble something about my phone.

"So you can be trained."

Oh no he didn't.

"Go screw yourself with a rusty fish fork." I'm not swearing, purposefully. This asshole isn't getting the pleasure of my lips around his probably giant cock—if the bulge in his pants is anything to go by. I'm a motherfucking queen at blow jobs, he has not earned one.

His low chuckle has me rolling my eyes, it sends an unwanted tingle to my clit, and it can fuck right off. He walks over to my bedside table and opens the drawer, and would you believe it? He finds both my phones.

"These what you're looking for, *Dolcezza*?" He holds them both up, that cocky eyebrow raised again, and a smirk on his stupidly beautiful face.

"Yes. Thank you." I hold out my hand for them, after barely getting the words *thank you* out of my mouth.

"An ass show, backing down, and now a thank you?" His tone is definitely sarcastic as he hands the phones over, but there's a hint of worry in his eyes too. "Must be my lucky day."

"Well, it's got to be someone's, and it certainly isn't mine, is it?" I meet his gaze again, pushing every ounce of hatred I have for this man out, praying for this job to be over quickly. I may have a contract with him, well, mostly, but that doesn't mean he gets to be a complete dick to me.

Agonizingly slowly, he runs his fingers through my hair, stopping to cup the back of my head in his hand. He holds me there, staring up at him. He surprises me by gently kissing my forehead before turning to walk away. As he opens the room door, he looks over his shoulder at me to speak. "Two minutes, *Dolcezza*." Then he leaves, closing the door behind him.

"Argh!" I let out a cry of frustration. For my situation, for Marco's asshole behavior... for Mr. Bobby's life.

Deep inhale, deep exhale.

Focus, River.

I turn my personal phone on and wait for it to load. After inputting my code, the phone comes to life and I immediately open my messages, just as Marco comes back in like an indoor hurricane.

"Doc said you can go home in the morning. Put these on." He throws some pink sweatpants and a plain white T-shirt on the bed next to me. They're fucking disgusting. I'm all for wearing what you like, but sweatpants—especially bubblegum pink ones—have never been a me thing. The clothes knock my hand, and my phone tumbles to the floor—thank fuck I invested in the super-clumsy-person case.

Marco bends to pick it up for me, and I could get used to seeing him on his knees, but I shake that thought away as he looks at my screen. His face changes from smug bastard, to downright feral.

"What the fuck is this, River?" Turning my screen to me, he shows me what has soured the atmosphere.

The text message.

And now I remember it.

That was supposed to be for you.

The bullet that killed Mr. Bobby was intentional, only it hit the wrong person. I mean, deep down, I know this.

I know it should be me in the morgue, but to have it confirmed like this sends a lump to my throat.

"Is this from the shooter?" His voice is so deep it's sending vibrations throughout my entire body.

I nod. Unable to speak through the blockage in my throat.

"Okay. I'll deal with it."

Just like that, I can breathe again, because this asshole can fix fuck all.

"What are you going to do? Put a hit out on him? We need to tell the police."

He raises that fucking brow at me again, as if to say, *yeah, and what are you going to do about it?*

"Seriously, Marco? Don't be ridiculous, this isn't the Godfather."

"I protect what's mine, *Dolcezza*. And for the next three to four months, that includes you."

Rolling my eyes, I lean back on the bed. "I am fake-yours."

He moves so fast, I almost slip backward, then he's in my face, his mouth at my earlobe. Taking it between his teeth, he bites down hard, making me squeal and pull away. Then he growls, deep and low before letting go and speaking.

"Get dressed, *Dolcezza*. I'll be back in five minutes."

And he's gone again. This dude's giving me whiplash.

I sigh, resigned to my current fate. I agreed to this, and I won't fail.

I don't fail.

Chapter Eight
River

I don't know how he did it.

Whether he used charm or force. Whether he lied or used loopholes. I suppose it doesn't really matter since the end result is the same. Marco had a cot brought in and pretended to sleep in the room with me.

I say pretended because anytime I moved, his eyes would pop open and, for a split second, I could see the worry etched on his features. It's like he cares or something. Why would he be such an asshole if that were the case?

To top it all off, two of his goons were parked outside my door like twin versions of Cerberus guarding the gates of Hell. Marco being Hades, of course.

As I open my eyes this morning, I turn to my side and briefly watch my long-term client before he realizes I'm awake. I didn't sleep much since the nurses were coming in and out at regular intervals to check on my concussion and to make sure I didn't fall into a coma—I think.

He's lying on his back, his suit jacket neatly folded over the hospital chair facing my bed and his shoes are under the chair like two good little soldiers. As my eyes travel down the length of his body, it occurs to me that his clothes aren't even wrinkled. How is that possible? Maybe he really is the mastermind of evil, able to subdue his wardrobe into doing his bidding.

I snort but am unable to keep the noise down, causing Marco to stir.

Taking this rare moment of peace and quiet, I reach over for my phone and check for any new messages or notifications. Three letters catch my attention. CAG.

Nathaniel tried to reach me, no doubt having heard about the shooting since it's all over the local news. He and Mr. Bobby had a bit of a man-bond going on; I can only guess he's grieving our loss as well.

It's the first time I've heard from him since he gave me the ultimatum, after my many attempts to speak to him. Except, this time, I'm the one ghosting him, simply because I have no idea what to tell him. How do I even explain my life right now?

"Sorry, Nathaniel. I know we had a connection but I've decided to marry some guy I barely know?" Yeah, that's not going to go over very well.

So, just like any other normal person, I procrastinate.

As if he knows exactly where I am at all times, Marco's head turns to the side and his piercing eyes find me immediately.

"How did you sleep?" There isn't a single hitch in his voice. No signs of sleep clogging his vocal chords.

"Like someone who's in a hospital with a concussion." We're staring at each other, unabashed and unwavering.

"Hmm, *bene*." Rising to his feet, he unfolds his lithe body with fluid moves that make me jealous. My limbs are heavy and my energy levels are next to nothing. Above all else, my heart feels like it's anchored to the ground with grief. I suppose the only thing bringing me a semblance of joy is watching Marco watch me, the contact breaking briefly as he slips his thousand-dollar shoes on with practiced ease.

Within two steps, he's at my bedside, my head tilted up so our gazes stay fixed to each other. Reaching out his hand, he runs his fingers through my hair until his palm holds the side of my head, his thumb running along the scar above my eyebrow. It hasn't completely healed yet, the jagged edge like an ugly reminder of my attack.

"Where did you get this?" His voice is low, intense, focused... just like him.

"I fell." I give him my standard response but my heart just isn't in it. It sounds as empty as my motivation right now.

Marco doesn't respond, his face an unbreakable mask, as he wills the truth from my lips with his stare alone.

"Fine. Goddamn it. I was attacked in an alley. Happy?" It's not that I'm pissed at him, I just don't want to have to talk about what happened. If I'm honest, I got lucky. If those kids—although the size of those guys was no joke—hadn't come around, I have no idea what would have happened to me.

It's only because I'm still looking at him that I notice the tightening of his jaw before he speaks.

"Happy?" His thumb runs over my eyebrow once more, his lips landing softly on my forehead. "No, *Dolcezza*. I'm enraged." Then he takes a step back, his gaze hopping from my scar, to my eyes, to my lips, and back to my eyes. "I'll grab us some coffee."

I watch him as he walks away, opening the door and stepping out before softly closing it behind him. The baritone of his voice is clear through the door, probably talking to his watchdogs. I hope he brings them coffee, too, since those poor guys didn't get a wink of sleep.

With a heavy sigh, I force my sore body to scoot up to a sitting position. For a few seconds, my head swims in fog before it clears. I need to get out of here, get back to my apartment so I can plan Mr. Bobby's funeral.

The thought makes my stomach clench and the unmistakable urge to vomit rises then falls. None of this makes any sense. I'm nobody. No one. Why would a bullet be meant for me? I've barely had five minutes to myself before a slew of white-coat-clad individuals enter my room.

"Good morning, Mrs. Mancini, I'm doct—" *Excuse me?*

"Ms. Fox."

"I'm sorry?"

"My name is River Fox, I'm not married."

"Yet." Marco's voice booms from the room's entrance, and when I narrow my gaze in his direction, I find him carrying two coffees and a self-satisfied grin.

"Right. Yes, Ms. Fox. We are a teaching hospital, would you mind if my interns present your case?" I look at each one of them, a total of five, then address the doctor.

"No, that's fine." Marco hands me my coffee—black with two sugars—and I'm equal parts pissed off that he would know these details about me and grateful that I didn't have to tell him.

"River Fox, twenty-six-year-old female admitted last night with a concussion from a blunt force to the head. She presented with nausea and vomiting. Dizziness and loss of balance, headache and fatigue. Following a first assessment, she slept for three hours. The most recent scans show no abnormalities to the brain, no swelling or displacement." The intern who looks like a baby genius barely breathes as he rattles off the last couple of days of my life like he's memorized for a test.

"You're good to go home, Ms. Fox. You need to take it easy, watch for any nausea and headaches you may continue to experience. If the symptoms get worse, please make sure to come back and see us. We'll have your discharge papers done within the next three hours. Do you have any questions?"

"Um, no. Thank you." I look to Marco who's calmly sipping his coffee and pretending like he's just casually hanging out. But that damn tick in his jaw is telling me a whole different story.

As quickly as they arrived, they were gone. To my surprise, a three-hour wait turned into only thirty minutes and I'm guessing Marco had something to do with that.

When I insisted on being taken back to my apartment, Marco was not a fan of the idea. I had to threaten him with bodily harm before he conceded and asked his driver to take us back to my place. The entrance to the building is taped off with the same yellow tape you see in the movies or TV shows. As per usual, the parking on our street is impossible so we double park just long enough to be dropped off.

"I'll call you when we're ready." Marco steps out of the car right behind me, taking my hand and pulling me into his body.

"You don't have to do this, *Dolcezza*. Just tell me what you need, I'll grab it and if I miss anything, I'll buy it for you." His hold is like steel, keeping me from moving toward the stoop where Mr. Bobby should be. Where a cup of coffee should be. Where a bottle of whisky would be if this were a normal day where Mr. Bobby hadn't literally jumped in front of a bullet. For me. Fuck, thinking about it hurts so much.

Reaching up, I wrap my fingers around his hand where it holds my other wrist and squeeze. It takes him a second but he finally relents with a heavy, frustrated sigh.

"Don't say I didn't warn you." His words are cruel but the bite is non-existent. Like he's playing a part without any conviction whatsoever.

My first step toward the scene is tentative, hesitant. Fearful.

My second step physically hurts.

My third step brings me close enough to see that the blood hasn't been scrubbed off. It's there, a stain on the cement and in my memories. A color forever synonymous with loss.

He died saving my life.

It's my fault he's dead.

I did this.

My breath hitches but I refuse to break down again. I need to organize the wake and the funeral because I know for a fact that he had no one. Everyone he loved is gone. And now, so is he.

As I reach the door, the flashbacks from that afternoon assault me.

The hug, the laughter, the yelling, the pain from my skull hitting the cement.

Biting my lower lip to stave off the tears, I look away, concentrating instead on every step until I reach my apartment door.

It's when I enter my private space, one that already has the bitter taste of invasion of privacy written all over it, that I completely lose my shit.

"Where's all my stuff?" How am I supposed to take it easy if Marco insists of making me fucking crazy?

"Most of it is in storage. Your personal belongings are in the bathroom." Yeah, we're going to have words over this.

"What the fuck, Marco? Who the hell do you think you are?" He doesn't step inside, instead he stands in the doorway like he owns the fucking block, his hands in his pockets, his features stoic.

"*Tsk tsk, Dolcezza.*" He's shaking his head as he flicks an imaginary piece of lint from his perfect suit that he slept in all night before he raises his eyes and pins me with a look that would make the devil cower. "What did I say about that mouth of yours?"

"Fuck, fuck, fuck, shit, cunt, fuck." I sound like a lunatic, my voice shrill, my hands shaking and before I know what's happening, I'm engulfed in the steel embrace of Marco's arms.

"The doctors said you needed to rest, which means you can't do everything yourself." He lets up just a little when I've started to calm down and looks me straight in the eyes. "Given the choice, would you rather take care of your grandpa's funeral or pack your shit?" I can't deal with this hot and cold treatment, and I'm pretty sure he's even giving himself a migraine.

"Please, don't make this out to be some kind act on your part. You're controlling and need things to be exactly as you want them." Fucker doesn't even pretend to disagree.

"*Sí*. I am controlling. I am domineering. I am all the things." Pinching my chin, he brings my face up to his. "And the reason I am all of these things is because I protect what's mine. I've told you, this, River. Don't make me repeat myself." With a quick kiss on the cheek, he steps away and just like that, he's back to being cold.

"Get your shit, you have a meeting with the grandpa's lawyer."

"What?"

The sigh he gives me reminds me of when my mother would get annoyed with my teenage antics. Like he's frustrated and exhausted all at once.

"I've arranged a meeting with Mr. Bobby's lawyer since he had important information for you."

"Why am I only hearing about this now? I appreciate the gesture and all but a little heads up would be appreciated." Marco's gaze is assessing, his eyes traveling around my face as though searching for more and nodding when he seemingly finds it.

"Duly noted." Those two little words feel like a victory.

"I mean, I get it. You're used to doling out orders and having everyone sprint to do your bidding, but I'm not that person, Marco. I've been on my own for too long to just be your doormat." As per usual, he's on me in a split second, large hands palming my face.

"If I wanted a doormat, I'd buy one that says 'fuck off'. And as far as you being alone? Those days are over. You stand beside me, not behind me." I smile at his words, at the sincerity echoing in every syllable. At the meaning between the lines and the expiration date in the full stop.

It takes me less than twenty minutes to grab what I need since everything non-essential was apparently packed away in storage. I'm so used to being the one who plans and takes care of business that it almost feels like an affront to be the one being cared for like this. But secretly, I'm grateful. Not that I'd ever tell him, his ego is big enough as it is.

With a backpack filled to the brim, I walk out of my room to find Marco in my kitchen, talking quietly on the phone. As if he can feel my presence, he turns to me and for a brief moment, the fire in his eyes has returned, but then he shuts it down like a machine, reverting back to his mother tongue.

"*Si. Trovalo e portalo da me... in ginocchio.*" I have no idea what he's saying but the heat in his words seems just as important as the command he gives. I don't need to understand the language to know he's given an order to whomever is on the other end of the line. It's obvious, despite his cool demeanor, when he disconnects the call.

"What did you say?"

"I'm having some food delivered to the house so you can eat while you go through the funeral home's options." He's lying to me. I have no idea how I know, I just do. Conveniently, I don't really give a fuck. I'm tired already, but more than that, I'm determined to give Mr. Bobby the best goodbye he could ever imagine.

Chapter Nine
River

The house we pull up in front of is unassuming and kind of disappointing. I was expecting a lavish spectacle of a home, with balustrades and electric gates and gargoyles on the spires. Okay, that may be a little far, but as Marco opens my door and offers me his hand to help me out of the car, the building we're standing before kind of blends in. It is directly opposite Central Park though, so I bet the views from the third-floor windows are something to behold, especially at sunset.

Marco's grip on my hand is firm as he taps the top of the black Lincoln before it takes off to fuck knows where. Probably a lair somewhere deep underground. I know the Mancini family is involved in some shady shit, which was—surprisingly—not something that I accounted for when making my decision to do this job. Although, I'm pretty sure I never completely agreed, it's more like I was bulldozed into it.

The front door opens as soon as we get close, and a short, white-haired Italian man stands in the doorway, his arms open wide.

"River, *bella mia*, so nice to finally meet you. Come give Stefano a hug."

We're close enough that he is able to take me by the arms and pull me in. He smells of nicotine, like he's smoked within the last few minutes. It's not the worst smell in the world, but it's also not my favorite. Marco's hand remains firm in mine, with my arms by my sides in the most awkward hug ever.

"Let me look at you." He holds me in front of him before pulling me in again to air-kiss either side of my face and letting me go. "Oh *si, Signore*, she is good. Luca made some fresh *taralli*, it is in your office. The lawyer arrived *due minuti fa*, and Vincenzo is keeping him company until your arrival. I told him hands off the *taralli*, that is for the lady of the house."

Stefano talks a mile a minute, his heavy Italian accent making it barely audible to my ears, but there's something about this little man that's endearing. He has a wonderful, happy energy. Completely opposite to the grumpy asshole holding my hand.

"*Grazie*, Stefano. Is everything else organized?"

"*Sissignore*. Exactly as requested." He has a glint in his eyes as they flicker to me briefly when he answers.

"*Bene*. Take the afternoon off, Stefano."

I don't see his face, but his tone is a lot lighter than the one he uses with me. Stefano bows his head slightly before turning and walking away. And holy mother of all that is beautiful, I'm only now noticing how grand this place looks. What looked like nothing but a few terraced houses on a busy street, is actually a humongous goddam mansion inside. I may be exaggerating again, but only slightly.

The walls are all white, but they're decorated with colorful pieces of art, which goes really well with the shiny black marble flooring. The splashes of color give the whole place a modern vibe, but in a really stylish way. I expected gaudy and showy, but I guess Marco isn't as predictable as I'd assumed.

"Ready, *Dolcezza*?"

"For what?" I turn to look at him, and his gray eyes are boring into mine. It's almost as if he's holding back from speaking. The intensity of his gaze says everything and nothing at all. "Are you going to answer me, or continue to stand there like a mute?"

His right eyebrow flicks up, and one corner of his mouth tilts in a semi-smile—if you can even call it that. It's more like a smirk.

"*Sei un peperino oggi*. The lawyer is waiting." He pulls me toward the stairs, practically dragging me behind him.

I still don't know how or why Marco has arranged this appointment, and I'm really not ready for it, but my choice has been taken away from me. I'm being thrown into the deep end with this shit, and those annoying fucking warm feelings come back.

"You don't need to pull my arm off, Marco. I can walk by myself. I've been doing it for the last twenty-six years, you know. I'm actually quite good at it." I try to gently untangle my hand from his grasp, but he doesn't let up.

"Considering the number of times you've *fallen*, I'd say you're not as good at holding yourself up as you thought." He speaks through gritted teeth and I turn to read his face, but I can only see his profile as he continues to lead me up the stairs.

Fucking asshole.

His words are like a punch to my gut.

"How fucking dare you."

He pauses at the top of the stairs and turns to look at me, something akin to hatred in his eyes. If I annoy him so much, I have no idea why he wants me to work for him in this way. But fuck it, it kinda makes it a little more fun for me, and that feeling of gut-wrenching pain inside me lightens a little at the knowledge.

"Oh, *Dolcezza*. I dare. The question is, do you?"

"You know I do. Or are you forgetting our little game at dinner the other night?" My gaze is challenging, and I'm focused on annoying the fuck out of this man rather than the lawyer who I'm sure is on the other side of the door we're now standing in front of.

Without answering or removing his eyes from mine, Marco opens the door and almost pushes me inside. I stumble, but only a little as I make my entrance with him following closely behind. Before I can turn to give the asshole a piece of my mind, a tall, athletic looking man stands from the deep-red couch by the wall and addresses Marco.

"Marco, this is Mr. Langley, the lawyer." The bald-headed lawyer stands and holds his arm out to shake hands with Marco, both giving each other a light nod as they do. His glasses rest on the tip of his bulbous nose like an old school teacher.

"Welcome, Mr. Langley. This is River Fox." Marco gestures to me, and Mr. Langley's eyebrows raise slightly, as if he's surprised to see me.

The nerves I was feeling before all come flooding back, but I do my usual, sliding my mask into place as I politely shake his hand with a smile.

"*Grazie*, Enzo. You may go, call me with any updates."

The tall man doesn't speak as he leaves, he doesn't even look my way. I don't think he even looked at me once, the whole time. Rude much?

"River, sit."

Oh my fucking good God. Does this man have no limits?

"I'm not a dog, Marco," I mutter just loud enough for him to hear as he stands beside me.

He sighs before placing a hand on my lower back and pushing me toward the large chair behind the fancy mahogany desk, his other hand on my hip. Just as I think he's about to sit me down in what is obviously his chair, he sits himself, and pulls me onto him. He holds me there with one hand resting on my stomach, and the other on my thigh.

Completely inappropriate for this kind of meeting, but again I'm thankful for the distraction for what I know is about to be a difficult conversation.

"Mr. Langley, please begin." Marco rubs small circles on my thigh with his thumb and fingers, and I feel like I'm holding it all together really fucking well right now.

I want to fight him and push him away from me. I want to avoid this conversation forever and a day. I want to erase the last year of my life and make new decisions. But then, I wouldn't be me.

The universe only deals out what it thinks someone can handle.

Though, I'm beginning to think the universe has misjudged me completely.

The note from Mr. Bobby that the lawyer handed over is staring up at me from the desk in front of us. Mr. Langley left a few minutes ago, and the office has been silent since. I'm in shock more than anything. The little Mr. Bobby had—his apartment and everything inside it—has been left to me, and his funeral is already paid for. He bought himself a plot next to his wife so they could be together in the afterlife.

All I have to do is agree to the date for the funeral and turn up on the day. But I can't leave it at that. Mr. Bobby deserves more than just me at his funeral. I need to do more for him.

My mind is swirling with sadness, regret, guilt, and I want to curl up in a ball and feel sorry for myself for a while.

"*Dolcezza?*"

Shit. I forgot he was there. Fuck knows how. I guess his small distractions have actually been a strange kind of comfort, allowing me to feel relaxed even though I want to break.

Closing my eyes, I take a deep breath. I'm working now. I'm being paid to do a job, and I'm thinking of the big picture.

I stand and turn to face Marco, sliding my hands down his shirt-covered chest, across his stomach, over his tenting pants, squeezing his thighs. I'm ready to get on my knees and allow myself to forget all the shit going on and just concentrate on doing what I do well.

Marco has other ideas. His eyes turn feral, his scowl full of desire as he grabs my hips and places my ass on the desk in front of him.

I'm getting fucking sick of people turning me down when I'm trying to forget my own mind. Leaning back on the desk, resting on my palms, I look to the ceiling, exasperated at the situation.

A low growl brings my attention back to Marco, and he grabs my knees, roughly spreading my legs in front of him.

Okay, so, I'm not being turned down. I smile at him, a real, genuine smile as I lean forward and place my hands on either side of his chiseled face, pulling his lips to mine for a rushed kiss with all the tongue. It's messy, and heated, and full of angry desire.

Marco's hands roughly massage their way up my bare thighs, pushing my deep-green tea-dress up as he goes. When he reaches my hips, he growls again as he tugs at the waistband of my lace thong.

He leaves my underwear behind as his hands move from my hips, up my sides, his thumbs pressing into my nipples before coming to a stop on either side of my face. With one final, hard suck of my tongue, he pulls away and pushes me backward with a hand on my chest, his fingers against my throat.

I fall back on my elbows as his hands and mouth work their way down my body. He stands from the chair and leans over me, squeezing my breasts in each hand. Sliding my dress down my shoulders, he frees my nipples, immediately taking one into his mouth and biting down hard enough to draw blood. It hurts, but at the same time, he's moved my thong to the side and is thrusting two fingers inside me, and a breathy scream escapes my throat at the pleasure-pain combination.

"You're so wet for me." He stands again, fingers still inside my pussy and his other hand tweaking at my nipple.

I look up at him through lust-filled eyes, wishing he'd just fuck me already. I need this.

"Are you going to just stand there, or are you going to do something about it?"

A dangerous smirk crosses his face, his eyes darkening, and he pinches my nipple, hard. I hiss through my teeth at the pain before he slides his fingers out of my pussy and rubs at my clit.

"Like this?" he growls.

"Fuck, yes. Just like that." I'm panting as he alternates from my clit to pushing his fingers back inside me, still pinching at my nipple and keeping eye contact with me.

An orgasm is building, and I'm so fucking close. Nobody has been quite this rough with my nipples before, and it's apparently my kryptonite. I'm on the cusp, that delicious tingling in my gut growing, until it stops.

What the fuck?

Marco places his hands to either side of me on the desk, pressing his face close to mine.

"What did I say about your language, *Dolcezza*?"

Oh no, he better not be stopping now.

"Oh come on, that surely can't count?"

He grins, and it can only be described as feral as he sniffs at my neck before whispering in my ear.

"Oh but it can, *Tesoro*. You smell so good, all wet and needy for me, but I warned you." As he speaks, he's slowly pulling my dress back up my arms, onto my shoulders and covering my nipples. "Luca has prepared a dinner. Let's go eat, then I will show you to our room. Don't get any ideas, though. I have work to do, so you'll be sleeping alone tonight, wondering if I'll come to bed and finish what I just started."

Taking my earlobe in his mouth, he bites down before sucking it, then stands, adjusting his huge cock screaming to get out of his pants. He pushes my legs back together, slowly, before walking over to the door and opening it, waiting for me to follow like a good little girl.

Fucking asshole.

Chapter Ten

Marco

"Here." Without looking at Enzo, I take his offered glass of Louis XIII cognac. At almost five thousand dollars a bottle, not a drop is wasted anywhere but on the tongue.

"*Grazie.*"

"Salute." Our sentiment is announced in unison, our eyes locked as per tradition, but my mind is upstairs in another room, with another guest in my home.

As I take a sip, I let the floral and candied fruit aromas take over my pallet, diffusing—little by little—the spices and ginger with a healthy dose of honey. But the best cognac in the world can't compare to the unique, heady, taste of River Fox. Just one taste and I'm already fucking addicted.

"No offense, but—" I cut him off right there. This discussion is getting old and my patience is wearing thin.

"Nothing good ever comes after that introduction, Enzo. Unless you want to live with the fish in the Hudson, I suggest you reel in your criticism." Sitting comfortably on my grandfather's favorite leather seat I had shipped from Gaeta, I let the warmth from the fireplace ease my tightly coiled muscles.

"All I'm saying, Marco, is that it's gonna be real fucking hard to go legit if you're chasing her demons all around The City." With my eyes fixed on the dancing flames, I slowly bring my glass to my lips and inhale the rich aroma.

"Don't worry about me." Forcing myself to slide my gaze from the fire to Enzo, I sit up—my elbows resting on my knees—and cradle my glass in the palm of my hand. "Did you do what I asked?"

"Not yet, but I'm close." The evil smile I feel curving up my lips reminds me that I'm a Mancini and using violence to avenge those in my inner circle is like oxygen to my lungs.

"Good. Like I said on the phone, I want him on his knees."

"*Bene.*" Enzo's right leg starts to shake up and down like he's nervous, except I've known him my entire life and I know he's trying to reel himself in before losing his composure.

"Just fucking say it, Enzo. Christ, you're making this cognac turn sour." I'd never hurt him, we both know this, unless he betrayed me—which he'd never do—but fucking hell, this conversation has run its course and I'm tired of explaining myself.

"Why are you so hung up on her?"

"I'm not."

Enzo scoffs and I want to throttle him for disrespecting me. "Watch yourself, brother."

"Elizabeth Ambrosio was more than willing to marry you. A good Catholic girl from Naples, her family loves you. Why are you spending your time with some girl who may or may not be who we—" Before he can finish that phrase, his throat is in my grasp, his breath held hostage by my fingers as they tighten around his windpipe.

Looking him straight in the eyes, I make myself perfectly clear.

"She's about to become my wife. You disrespect her, you disrespect me. *Hai capito?*"

"I understand perfectly." Any other man would have cowered under my attack but Enzo has seen me do worse, his broken nose back in senior year of high school being one of them.

We stare each other down for a beat before I let him go and pat him on the side of the face like my father often does with me.

"You're the brother I never got, Enzo. I need you to have my back."

"Always."

Glancing up at the stairs, I talk myself out of running up there and making River come so hard her screams are imprinted in the memory of the walls. She thinks this is a punishment, but she couldn't be further from the truth. It's so much more than that.

The pain she's feeling right now is destroying her self-confidence, it's playing with her level head. I know very little, but I do know this... I may be paying River to step in as my wife, but I'm not paying her to suck my dick because it's her job.

When we fuck, it'll be because she can't take another minute without my dick in every one of her welcoming holes.

The next morning, I make sure Luca, my cook, has a healthy and balanced breakfast ready for River so I can bring it up to her room. I'm giving her the space she needs, for now, before moving her into my room.

"Marco! Mamma said you're going to a funeral?" I hear my little sister before I see her as she hurriedly makes her way to me, heels clicking along my black marble floors. "Who died?"

We both stare at each other like deer in headlights. Her, because I'm halfway up the stairs carrying a tray with an array of foods, and me, because… well, for the exact same reason. This isn't normal. I don't bring women breakfast in bed. I never have and didn't think I ever would. Apparently, you can teach old dogs to heel.

"What are you doing?" Her words are whispered as though she's afraid that saying them out loud would disintegrate the image in front of her.

"Mind your own business, Lina. I can be a gentleman." At this, she outright laughs. A full belly laugh that has my molars grinding with the insult.

"I can't believe you're saying that with a straight face. Is that long-standing room you have booked at our Upper West Side location your way of being a gentleman?" Fucking brat. I ignore her and walk my ass to River's room where I hope I'll get a little more gratitude. Why do the women in my life make it a point to piss me off all day, every day?

Holding the tray with one hand, the only warning River gets before I walk straight into her bedroom is a double knock on the door. I'm feeling generous this morning.

Everyone in her life coddles her, makes her feel like she can't take on her own battles.

Fuck that.

Her backbone is made of titanium. She doesn't need protecting because *she's* the protector.

Until I came into the picture. I will push her until she's standing proud like the queen she is about to become.

"Rise and shine, *Dolcezza*." Placing the tray on the small table next to her bed, I walk straight to the curtains and pull them apart, letting the cloudy December day spill into the room.

When I turn around, I'm greeted with a thong-clad ass facing me and the rest of River's body hidden by the voluptuous down comforter. She apparently got lost in it during the night.

"River!" Fuck me, the things I want to do to that ass.

"Hmmm, your bed is the most comfy of all the beds in the world." Scratch that. The sleepy sound of her voice makes me want to do filthy things with her mouth even more.

"Get up."

"I don't wanna."

"River."

"Marco." She pauses then giggles. "Polo."

I'm quick as I lean in and slap her ass hard enough to make her jump and fall to the floor.

"What the fu—"

"Good girl, now eat."

By the time we make it to the car, the sky is threatening to unleash buckets of rain. The clouds are gray and heavy, the air is colder than usual. It'd be better if we got snow, but the temperatures, low as they are, just aren't cold enough.

River looks stunning in her black knee-length pencil skirt and black silk shirt, her hair adorned with a silver clip, her pearl earrings demure and sophisticated. Her black stilettos make her legs look endless, and I have visions of her digging those heels into my back as I fuck her into oblivion. I haven't seen her cry yet but her mind is far away, somewhere in the past with her departed friend.

Reaching over, I squeeze her thigh hard enough to get her attention.

"Hmm?" Turning to face me, her eyes are still glazed over but I want her attention solely on me.

"I will be there every step of the way. You lean on me when you need me, *Dolcezza*. Because that's what family does." That gets her attention.

"Family?" She scoffs like it's the most ridiculous notion in the world.

"Yes, River. Family. You've taken care of your brother and that useless excuse for a best friend," I mumble under my breath, "best friend my ass," then resume my short monologue. "Now, you're part of the Mancini family. We take care of each other. *I...*" My hand shoots out and grabs her chin so she's forced to look at me. "Take care of *you*. *Capito*?" I know she doesn't understand Italian but she'll have to at least know that, so I repeat myself. "Do you understand?"

"Yes." For the first time since this whole thing started, her eyes are clear and her answer is honest.

"*Bene*."

When we arrive at the plot where Bobby instructed his lawyer to place him, there's a half-moon crowd of people waiting around the open grave. A small wave of black dresses and suits with white handkerchiefs dabbing at their watering eyes.

River is at my side, her shoulders shaking more and more as we approach the gathering. Placing a hand at the small of her back, I rub a soothing thumb to remind her I'm here.

"You can sit at the front, he considered you his only family." At any other time, she'd be curious about how I know this, but instead of questioning me, she gives me a small smile. I have a feeling this is the only time I'll get the docile River of today. And as much as I'm enjoying it, I have to admit I prefer fiery River any day of the week.

At eleven on the dot, the pastor begins his celebration of Bobby's life and I tune him out, my attention fully on the figure standing diagonally behind me. He's angled in just a way that River can't see him, but he's clear in my line of sight.

I can see him gritting his teeth as his eyes virtually drill a hole into my hand as it rests on River's hip. I wait until he looks up then narrow my gaze at him.

I know he's up to something. I fucking hate that he's here, but there's nothing I can do about it without exposing myself as well.

A small sob escapes River and not a second later she's burrowed into my shoulder, my arms now fully around her. We stand there as Bobby's casket is slowly lowered into the ground and wait for everyone to walk up and drop a handful of dirt into the grave. Some pick up a rose and drop it as well. Following River's lead, I just stand there waiting for her to go whenever she's ready.

Inevitably, we come face to face with one of my closest friends growing up.

"Nathaniel?" River gasps, quickly jumping back and severing our connection.

The motherfucker doesn't even pretend to hide the smirk on his face.

"I wanted to pay my respects." Now it's my turn to grind my teeth as River crashes into Nate and wraps her arms around his neck as he holds her around the waist, his nose nuzzling her neck.

I want to rip his head right off his fucking shoulders for touching what's mine. For making her believe he's her comfort place.

He's not.

Once they separate, I pull her back into my space, bringing her hand up to my mouth to kiss off his touch. It's only an added bonus that it happens to be the hand sporting a huge fucking rock that says, "Marco Mancini's fiancé."

As his eyes land on the ring, I get a sick sense of satisfaction. Fucker needs to walk away.

"I see you've been busy." The unmistakable jolt of shock from River is like a match to a puddle of gasoline. It's swift and it's violent.

In one step I'm face to face with Nate, our eyes level, our shoulders ready for battle. "I think you've forgotten your manners."

"I think you've forgotten your place, *brother*." I ignore the malice resonating in that last word. The years of resentment it holds in every letter.

"Go home, Nate. Now's not the time and definitely not the place." My voice is steady despite the buzzing, savage fire burning just below my skin. The silence brewing between us is filled with memories of young boys with their whole futures ahead of them, friends whose turf was the privileged streets of the Upper East Side, planning the takeover of the world and splitting it three ways.

But devastating circumstances got in the way, which is the only reason I'm giving him an out. Out of respect for the years we spent as chosen brothers, I'm giving him an easy out so I don't have to kill him with my bare hands.

Our connection is severed as he turns to River and flashes her the charming, good-guy smile that got him laid so many times. It's always been the ace up his sleeve. We used to call it the Reed Effect.

By the softening of River's eyes, I'd say it's working on her, too. Her work ethic and respect for our contract is keeping her from melting at his feet like I've seen so many other women do throughout the years.

But then River has always been different. Unique in the way she carries herself. Reacts to others.

In the way she resists me.

"I'll see you later, Skittles."

Motherfucker. I may just throw away every memory I have of him for that little stunt, but I know how to control myself.

Barely.

I realize I'm vibrating with pent up, murderous energy when I flinch as River's hand lands on my bicep, gently pushing me out of her way.

"Marco, please." Her gaze bores a hole through my soul before she turns her attention to Nate again and to my horror, apologizes to him.

"I'm sorry, Nathaniel. I'll call you, okay?" Nate leans down, darting a cocky smirk my way that only I can see before a barely chaste kiss on the corner of her mouth. It's River's nails digging into the muscles of my arm that keep me in check and save me from making a scene at Bobby's funeral.

Bet he's looking down on us and wondering what the fuck is wrong with us.

Nate steps back and just before he walks away, he throws his last punch.

"See you around, Capo."

We watch him as his figure slowly moves away from us, and it's not until he's far enough that I can't distinguish his broad shoulders from his lean waist that I turn back to River.

During our quick altercation, those in attendance have dispersed—going back to the daily happenings in their lives—while River tries to recenter herself in a world where her dear friend no longer exists.

"You ready, *Dolcezza*?" Reaching for her hand, I roll my eyes as she slaps my touch away. Here we go again. What is it with this woman? All I ask is that she listen and do as I say.

"What the fuck was that?" I arch a brow at her language.

"One." She knows exactly what I'm talking about. And to be clear, I don't actually give a fuck that she talks like a biker raised on the city streets. What I do love is that my chastising her stokes her fire.

"Fuck you, Marco. Don't play this 'no cursing' bullshit. What the actual fuck was that whole..." she twirls a finger around where Nate used to stand then aims her pointer at me. "Gossip Girl episode?" I genuinely have no idea what she's talking about.

"Gossip Girl, Marco. The television show?" Still nothing.

"Oh my God, you're hopeless. It doesn't matter anyway. What was that? Tell me right now or the deal is off." Staring at her, I try to judge her bluff. Would she really walk away from five million dollars just to satisfy her curiosity?

Her right foot steps back, her eyes fixed on mine.

"One." It's her turn to give me an ultimatum and fuck me, I do not renegotiate terms already signed and sealed, which is why I stand my ground.

Her left foot joins her right and she's now too far from me, her hand falling away from my arm.

"Two." Every one of my muscles is tight, ready to uncoil like a viper feeling attacked.

Her body begins to turn as though she can walk away from me and live to tell her story but before she can call out the number three, I'm the one wrapping my fingers around her bicep, pulling her tightly to me.

"Do you know what happens to people who defy me, River?" My tone is lethal, my words never truer.

"Let me guess." Her words are venomous. "They end up at the bottom of the Hudson? Really, Marco? I've had a lot of words for you in my head but a cliché wasn't one of them." Leaning in, she's close enough that her scent is making my dick harder than the cement slab at River's feet.

"Hmm," looking around the area, I spot an oak tree standing proudly at the entrance of the forest, like a natural bouncer keeping the humans away.

But no one can stop me. I'm done playing and River needs to understand a few things.

"Hey! Where are you taking me?"

I answer, "You'll see soon enough."

Practically pushing her heeled feet into the ground, disrupting the patches of grass as I pull her away from any prying eyes, I stop when all we can see is brown from the trunks and deep green of the firs.

"This is ridiculous! Are you planning on making me disapp—" Her words are caught in her throat as I whirl around on her and slam myself against her front as her back meets the ragged edges of the trunk's surface.

"We have rules for a reason, *Dolcezza*. Contracts that are signed, limits that are established. For the next three months you are mine. You're not pretending and you're not part-time. You are fully, completely, and unequivocally mine." Pressing harder against her soft curves, my fingers find the hem of her skirt and with every word that passes through my lips, I bare an inch of her skin.

Every one of my senses is on high alert as I memorize her tells, those little hiccups and gasps that make me want to bury my dick all the way to the hilt until the only thing she knows is how good I make her feel.

"I didn't agree to that." The earlier venom is gone. In its place, her words are barely audible, needy. Her chest is rising and falling in rhythm with the staccato of her breaths. Up. Down. In. Out.

I own every inhale. I'd kill for every one of her exhales.

Once my fingers reach her panties, I bring my mouth to hers without touching her. It's just a whisper against her skin but it's enough to make a liar out of her. Her words are denying her need but her body is a fountain of untold truths.

"Are you angry?" Her eyes narrow at my question, the change in subject too sudden for comfort. Good. I want her on unsure footing.

"Yes, I am. You're an asshole." I push one finger inside her wet, hot cunt and curl the tip just enough to make her gasp and throw her head back against the wood.

"Try again."

"You… make me… angry." A second finger joins the first, pushing in until they can go no further, caressing her walls as they move in and out. This earns me a beautiful moan that I wish I could bottle up and carry with me everywhere I go.

"Wrong answer."

"Fuck, Marco. Yes, I'm angry. You… oh, God. More!" My thumb rubs against her clit, making her melt right into me.

"Why are you angry, River?" My words have a bite to them but she needs this, she needs to let go of it all.

"Yes! I'm fucking livid, okay? Someone killed him and it's my fault! I did this, goddammit!" Fucking finally.

Aiming straight for her g-spot, I give her the reward she deserves and watch, enthralled, as she collapses and cries through her orgasm, her cum coating my fingers and almost making me come in my pants. But I'm not quite done yet, palming her panties back into place, I make sure to soak up every ounce of her cum.

"Off."

"What now?" She knows exactly what I'm talking about, she's just being a brat. It's her default setting.

"Don't make me repeat myself. I want my trophy."

"Well, you paid for them, so it's no skin off my back." With a light shrug of her shoulders, she pulls down her panties and balls them up. She thinks she's being a bitch by throwing them at my face, but I revel in it, holding them to my nose as I inhale deeply, the sweet scent of her making me wish I'd buried my dick inside her.

She raises a brow at my antics, and I make a show of licking her panties before putting them in my pocket.

I've got her now, right where I want her.

Right where she needs to be.

Chapter Eleven
River

While I'm well aware that I've flipped my own world on its axis by agreeing to this contract with Marco, it couldn't have come at a better time. It's been three days since Mr. Bobby's funeral, and yes, it still hurts like a bitch to think about what happened, but Marco has kept me so busy, it's kept my overwhelming emotions at bay.

Going shopping for new clothes the day after felt all kinds of wrong, but when Marco insisted we stop for an Irish coffee break, I couldn't help but smile at the memories the drink gives me. Mixing caffeine with liquor will always be something that makes me think of the beautiful soul that was my friend. As I took my first step, I remembered his words, his spirit, and I felt like the universe was sending me a sign. A sign that it's okay for me to carry on living, being happy, looking at the big picture. It was a proper Petal moment—which then made me feel guilty for not spending Winter Solstice with them, but they had understood what I needed to do. There's no way in Hell I'd miss a family event like that without a good reason.

The whole Nathaniel thing is getting to me as well. For the first time in forever, I had something for myself and I fucked it all up by allowing him to walk away. I could've chased him, I could've made more effort than I have been with a small text here and there, but I just haven't. And that's on me. I know it makes me a shitty person, but with everything else that's happened, some things just feel insignificant right now. Maybe when all this is over, I can pick my life back up and see what happens.

"Do you understand what is expected of you tonight?" As usual, Marco enters the bedroom without a knock or semblance of noise to warn me of his presence.

"Look pretty, smile, and worship the ground you walk on?" Sarcasm is my default mode when my insecurities get the better of me.

"Don't be cute, River, it's not becoming." Asshole.

"Fine. I'm about to become the big boss man's wife so classy, no cursing, and smiling. Is that better?" My fingers run down the silky fabric of the dress he's laid out on the bed and I can't help but throw some snark at him. "One thing is for sure, no one's getting fucked, apparently."

Every morning since being here, I've woken up alone. Marco still has yet to fuck me, or allow me to fuck him, and it's starting to piss me off. I suppose I shouldn't complain too much, as I've still been getting all the orgasms. At least twice a day, and at the most random times, Marco has either eaten me out or finger-fucked me to within an inch of consciousness. I haven't needed to use my lube on the pretense of being wet at all. It's like I'm in a constant state of arousal around this man and all he has to do is crook his finger and summon me. I have no fucking clue *why* my body responds to him the way it does, he's an asshole and pisses me the fuck off most of the time, but it is what it is and I try not to look too much into it.

I'm just fulfilling my end of the contract, and if he needs to give me orgasms... who am I to stop him?

"You'll wear the red dress I have laid out for you. Hair and make-up will be arriving in thirty minutes. Shower and wait in this room until I come for you."

"Oh, so it does work?" Considering I'm yet to even see this man's dick, I couldn't resist the cum reference.

"Behave."

"Always." I bat my eyelashes sweetly, just catching Marco's smirk as he shakes his head and leaves the room.

Tonight is the big Christmas Eve party—apparently, it's a big bash thrown by the Mancini family every year—and I'm not exactly ecstatic about it. Going to all the galas and things with Tyler was something I enjoyed, but I had a lot more control. I knew what I was walking into, I had done all my research thoroughly, and I knew Tyler well enough to figure out his moods and how to handle them—usually with mindless sex. This evening, I don't feel like I have any of that control. I can't even pick my own fucking outfit.

"Here you go, *Signorina*. No Champagne."

Luckily, I've got Stefano on my side with his cocktail-making magic. Somehow, he's figured out my aversion for Champagne and created a special drink called "The Rose." I'd bet my nest-egg he's Marco's "guy" because for a house manager, he knows way too much. I'd go as far as saying I'm proud, and a little jealous of all his research sources.

"What would I do without you, Stefano?" A couple of sips are all I need to boost my morale.

"Probably get into a lot of trouble." Funny guy. Although he has a point. The time spent chatting with Stefano is time I'm not getting into trouble with Marco.

Maybe.

Marco had given me a list of last-minute things to shop for yesterday—though I suspect it was just busy work to keep me out of his hair—so I decided to put my own spin on it.

I managed to pick out a box of After Dinner Willies from online to go with the coffee being served following the meal this evening. I had the choice between dicks and nipples, but the nipples were too subtle. Luca found it just as funny as Stefano and me when they arrived and I took them into the kitchen. He even promised he wouldn't swap them out for something 'more appropriate' when he sends them out with the servers—like the sensible alternative of square shaped after-dinner mints. I'm well aware that it's immature as fuck, but also fucking funny. Seeing Marco's face this evening when he realizes what I did is what's getting me through this shit-show.

"Probably, but you know it's going to be epic."

"I know nothing, *Signorina*. I'm leaving now." He winks at me as he walks to the door. "Everything you need is here and someone will come up to help you get ready in just a bit."

I toy with the idea of finding something a lot more revealing to wear, just to be a brat and fuck with Marco, but the red one is actually quite nice.

Barely out of the shower and with a soft bath towel wrapped around my still-damp body, a knock on the door drags me from my thoughts. Before I have a chance to speak or even move, the golden handle turns and in walks one of the most glamorous women I've ever seen. She has the same stunning gray eyes as Marco, though hers are a lot friendlier, and her dark hair falls in waves against her shoulders.

"River! Oh my god, I can't believe I'm finally meeting you. I've been away for a few days with some friends, the Bahamas were calling to me. New York at Christmas is great and all that, but there's nothing like bikinis and cocktails on the beach. I left the day my brother brought you here or I would have totally come to say hey. But I'm here now, so we can have all the girl time. It's been so long since another woman has been in this house. It's like testosterone city up in here half the time. Oh, I'm Madelina by the way, but you can call me Lina, I prefer it, sounds less like an old Italian lady. So, whip that towel off your head and let me see what I'm working with!"

Wow, that's a lot to unpack. Madelina—Lina—talks a mile a minute, barely taking a breath between sentences. I get the impression she's a little nervous and trying to overcompensate, which is something I completely understand. So I take pity on the poor thing and give her a full-on smile.

"It's great to finally meet you too, Lina." Not that I knew Marco even had a sister, but I don't want to hurt her feelings by letting her think her brother hasn't mentioned her. "You're right about all the peen around here. It's definitely dick central."

She laughs, and it's the cutest sound as the worry in her eyes decreases. "Thank God you're not a prude. I don't know what I would've done with a prude for a sister-in-law." Placing herself on the bed next to me, she sighs and drops her eyes to her shoes—strappy golden stilettos showing off her perfectly manicured toes.

"Are you okay?" It's like she has something to say, but she's not sure if she wants to.

With a deep breath, she sits up straight and turns her head to face me, plastering a fake smile I know all too well on her face.

"I am, yeah. Sorry, I was just thinking... but we have all the things to do, so no time for all that. Towel. Off. Show me the hair." She swirls her finger around at my head before just ripping the towel away, leaving my damp strands to fall over my eyes. "Ooh, short. I like it, it's funky and brave. Okay, go sit at the vanity, and we'll get this styled, our makeup ladies will be here real soon."

"You're doing my hair?" I'm confused, because Stefano said there were people coming to do that—not that I need someone else to do these things for me, because I'm a grown-ass fully-capable woman. I was even thinking of sending the hair lady away when she arrived, but I like Lina. She gives off good vibes, so I move over to the vanity with Lina close behind.

"I am. I insisted because I wanted to meet you and have an actual conversation with you before the party starts. And Marco finds it hard to deny his baby sister anything, so he agreed. I did a course at college and the family helped me open a salon, but it basically runs itself with all the staff, so I barely get an opportunity to actually do hair anymore."

"Whoa, slow down. I've had too many of these cocktails to follow." I laugh, watching her in the mirror as she fingers my hair, head cocked to the side like she can already see her handy work.

"Sorry, I'm nervous. It's not like Marco ever brings any women around and when you're a Mancini, trust doesn't come easy. Hence my limited circle of friends. Which now includes you." Her grin is infectious.

"I'll drink to that." Holding up my fancy martini glass, I jump out of my skin when Stefano comes in, another cocktail in hand for Lina.

"*Grazie*, Stefano."

"*Prego*, Madelina."

I need a personal translator for these people with all their Italian going on.

"I thanked him and he said 'you're welcome'. Don't worry, we're not plotting your demise." Lina giggles at what I'm guessing is some kind of mob joke.

"To new friends and new sisters." I like the idea of having someone new in my life that I can hang out with.

We could even stay in touch once my contract with Marco is over.

Nope... no, I can't do that. That goes against everything I know I should be doing. When a contract terminates, being friends with their family after the fact isn't something I can allow.

"Let's get to it then." She claps her hands together in excitement, like she's about to play with her favorite toy.

Fun times.

"Oh my God! You look unbelievable, River!"

Lina, in all her sparkling golden glory, isn't wrong. She did an amazing job styling my hair, it's got more volume than I've ever been able to do myself, and the longer strands are in cute swirls framing one side of my face. The red diamond drop earrings are all the jewelry this outfit needs. It feels like I'm wearing nothing, yet I'm fully covered from neck to feet in red silk. The high neck is adorned with crystals, which flow out like raindrops to barely nothing at the bottom of the fishtail skirt. My arms are covered in a soft, sheer, red material, also dotted with crystals, and the side panels around my waist match. The slit that reaches mid-thigh is needed or I'd be walking like a penguin all evening with how fitted the dress is. It shows every curve and I love it.

My red satin Jimmy Choo's are decorated with a delicate crystal chain around my ankle, with more crystals dripping down the line of my heel. They're like jewelry and shoes all at once. For the first time today, as I stand in front of the floor-length mirror, I feel like I might actually have a good time this evening. I mean, who wouldn't when they feel like a fucking goddess?

Though I'm certainly not the only goddess in this room; Lina is like an actual Greek Deity. Without makeup, she was already stunningly beautiful, with it, she's like a whole new woman. Fierce and ready to take names in her floor-length golden gown.

"And you are breathtaking, Lina. Honestly, your brother is going to flip his shit when he sees you."

She blushes and waves away my compliment. As the oldest sibling in my own family, I completely understand how difficult it is to walk that fine line between protecting and allowing them their independence. Although, I'm probably erring on the side of too much protection still, but that's not a today's me problem.

"You know what, I really like you. Please don't let my brother's macho bullshit scare you away. He can be intense, but he has a good heart."

I try my hardest not to scoff at her statement.

"I like you too, Lina. And don't worry about me, I can handle your brother." With a sip of my cocktail, I give her a friendly wink.

"I don't know, River. His grumpy meter has been on high alert lately. It's his first year organizing the Christmas Eve party." My brows furrow at that little bit of information. It's like I'm starving for more when it comes to this man.

"Is it, really?" He seems so in control, I'm surprised he hasn't been planning since birth.

"Yeah, our great-grandparents started the tradition and until last year, my parents were hosting. But with your wedding coming up, it's now Marco's responsibility."

Well, that's just my luck, isn't it?

"On that note, I'm going to get my ass downstairs and into the hall before he can stop me." She giggles and shrugs her shoulders. "Are you a hugger? Can I hug you? I'm a hugger, sorry."

"Don't you dare apologize for that. And never ask me again, I insist you give all the hugs whenever you like. Okay?"

My cheeks hurt so much already from smiling for the last couple hours with Lina. Despite all the money and privilege, I think Petal would like her.

Lina basically attacks me, wrapping her arms all the way around me. She's a little shorter than I am, and I hold her as hard as she's holding me—anything less would be pretty shitty and Petal would have my ass for lack of effort. I feel like I need this as much as Lina.

Not going to allow my thoughts to go down that route though, tonight is about putting on that all-important mask I wear so well, and maybe a little bit of penis choco-late.

"See you downstairs, I have to wait until your brother summons me."

"Okay, I'll see you down there." She claps her hands together, her excitement not quite as infectious as I'd like, before air kissing both of my cheeks and exiting the room the way she'd entered earlier; like a whirlwind.

Any other time, I would completely defy Marco's orders and head downstairs without waiting for him, but there are going to be a lot of people here and I need to be what Marco is paying for.

Ten minutes later, Marco enters the room, and holy mother of all hot men, a tux looks good on him.

He stands in the doorway for a moment, his eyes caress-ing my body; from my toes, up my one exposed thigh, over my chest and landing on my face. His gray eyes seem to swirl with desire, which makes me smile internally—okay, externally too—before he nods once and his jaw seems to harden.

"*Bene.* Let's go, *Dolcezza.*" He turns and holds out his elbow for me to take, and I do, allowing him to lead me from the room and down the staircase.

Mr. Talkative remains silent the whole way, pausing briefly to adjust his jacket by the hall doors, which are currently being manned by some heavy-looking security guys.

"Best behavior tonight," is all he says as he nods for one of the men to open the door for him to make his grand entrance.

"Sir, yes sir."

He responds to that with a growl, moving my hold on his arm so that our hands are clasped together as we walk in. I plaster on my smile, ready to greet the masses.

Chapter Twelve

River

The hall is beautiful, a touch of the old-fashioned mixed with the modern, gold and marble accents throughout the room. It's decorated with Christmas trees, sparkling lights, and enough round tables to seat a hundred people. Each table has a different Christmas-themed centerpiece on a white tablecloth, and the people are all dressed in their finery. It's a lavish event, no doubt a lot of posturing and business deals will happen this evening.

Christmas isn't something my family and I usually celebrate in the traditional sense, Winter Solstice—also known as Yule—is our thing. And though I missed the beginning on the 21st, it lasts for twelve days, so as soon as all this Christmas faff with Marco is done with, I'll be visiting my family for a few days. Luckily, it's something I had written into our contract, because I'm positive Marco wouldn't let me leave if I hadn't. He's had my schedule meticulously planned for the last few days, and I need a break from it already.

Several stuffy old men have come to greet Marco on our entrance, all the hand shaking and wishes for happy holidays given before we move onto the next. I smile politely, nod at the right moments, and say how wonderful it is to meet them.

The next couple we greet are obviously Marco's parents. Mr. Mancini looks like an older version of Marco, a few more wrinkles and darker skin, his hair graying on the sides. He has kind, brown eyes, but I get dangerous vibes from him, like he could flip a switch any moment. Mrs. Mancini is like a vision in white. Her eyes are the same color as her children's, a beautiful stormy gray, and she looks like the kind of lady that could tell a few stories.

Marco holds his mom by the shoulders and air kisses both of her cheeks before moving on to his dad.

Mrs. Mancini's face drops as I come to stand in front of her, and it's like she's just a ghost or something. Her eyes glaze over as if she's lost in a memory of the past.

"My God. It's uncanny." Mrs. Mancini air kisses my cheeks, and confuses the fuck out of me with her reactions. "Look, Alberto. Doesn't she loo—?"

"Mamma, not now." Marco kisses his mom on the cheek before grabbing me by the waist and practically dragging me away from them. I have so many questions, but this isn't the time or place to ask them. I'll just have to file them away for later, when I'm not trying to be the good little fiancé.

Lina and Vincenzo are at our table, and a few other serious-looking men I have no interest in getting to know. The meal goes well, and Lina is sitting next to me, thank fuck, because I'd be bored out of my mind otherwise. Marco's hand never moves from my bare thigh, rubbing small circles with his thumb as he makes polite conversation with one of the men—I'm assuming some kind of boss to the others. Vincenzo is sitting next to Lina and he remains stoic as ever. I have yet to see him crack a smile. I'll work on that, my own mini-mission to make Enzo smile.

The meal is delicious, I don't remember ever having so much food. Fish for a Christmas eve dinner is unusual to say the least, but Lina told me it's an Italian tradition. It's surprisingly satisfying, although I'll probably be hungry again in an hour. And now, the coffees are being brought out, and I have to stifle a giggle as Lina nudges me when she notices what the servers are carrying into the room—I may have mentioned my little coffee treat surprise to her, and she's just as excited as me to see her brother's reaction.

Small silver platters are placed on the tables containing cream, sugar, and the after-dinner mints. There are soft murmurs and the occasional stifled laugh as the platters are placed on tables around the room, and I smile to myself, enjoying the effect my own little stamp on the evening is having.

"What is this, Marco? Is this some kind of joke?" The grumpiest man at our table doesn't seem happy about the penis chocolate… oh well, he'll get over it.

I prepare myself for Marco's outburst of anger as Lina can't contain her giggles next to me. My face is as neutral as I can possibly make it in this moment, the old guy's reaction making my job harder because his outrage is bringing out my immature inner child.

"Thought I'd liven up the dinner a little. These things can be so monotonous, you know?"

Marco's reaction is unexpected, and he squeezes my thigh under the table, then slowly slides his hand up to my pussy and taps it a couple of times, before moving back to my thigh. Turning to look at him, I see a brow arched in amusement, and eyes that promise retribution. I shrug my shoulders and wink, then reach over to the chocolates and take one. We keep eye contact as I flick the tip of the chocolate dick with my tongue, then I slowly suck on the end just before I bite down, leaving just the chocolate balls in between my fingers.

The corners of Marco's lips tilt upward, and he shakes his head in amused disbelief before turning back to his guests. The old guy without a sense of humor sneers at me.

"*Quella non è della famiglia.*"

"Eric. Disrespect for my fiancé will never be tolerated." Marco's tone is calm, even, but the way his hand fists on top of my thigh tells a whole other story.

"What did he say?" I try to be discreet as I lean in and whisper to Lina.

"He said you're not part of the family." Her reply is as quiet as my question.

"But he's not family either, is he?"

Lina side eyes me, a hint of a smirk on her lips. "He doesn't mean it like that."

I'm so confused, but I don't have time to ask more questions before Eric's suddenly subdued voice catches the table's attention.

"There was no disrespect, Marco." The creep laughs nervously, but I can see the slight shake in his hand as he speaks. "All in good fun, right, boys?" He's addressing the silent guys to either side of him now.

They don't laugh. Their eyes are firmly on Marco, waiting for his next reaction.

It's actually kind of exciting.

Marco looks up to Vincenzo, who has moved like the silent ninja everyone in this fucking house seems to be and is now standing behind this self-entitled Eric dude. The man's smile fades as he feels Enzo's presence behind him, and he snaps his fingers, causing the three men with him to stand.

"Marco, come on. We're just having a good time. It's Christmas Eve."

The slow grin that crosses Marco's face is full of danger; I like it, but I don't think Eric does. His smug features dissolve into something close to confusion as Marco nods his head, ever so slightly, prompting Enzo to pull Eric up by his collar.

The man is spluttering in disbelief at what's happening, looking to his goons for help. They don't.

"Get. Out." The words are a deep rumble, and Marco squeezes my thigh, hard.

The blood falls from Eric's face and he goes pale, his features blank with shock before he finds just enough strength to speak.

"You're going to regret this." It's said under his breath, but audible enough.

In response, Marco laughs; a deep, evil kind of laugh that has all kinds of flutters happening in my panties. So, I guess I'm a little fucked up, but hey ho!

Ever the silent warrior, with a hand still on Eric's collar, Enzo begins to lead him away. The bodyguards surrounding him close in, but one look in their direction from Vincenzo, and they back off, allowing him to do his job. The three of them quietly follow their fallen master from the room, leaving Lina, Marco, and me at the table alone.

Though the interactions were all quiet and between our table, it's obvious to the rest of the room that something has occurred with the way Eric is being escorted out. No one is looking directly at us, but I can sense the whispered questions and the wary atmosphere. The only sounds coming from the low background music as everyone pretends nothing nefarious is happening.

Well, I never expected my penis chocolate to have this effect on the evening, and I kinda feel a little bad about it—only a little.

"*Dolcezza*," Marco whispers into my ear as he sits back down. "I'm going to spank your ass for that trick, but I can't deny it was fun and has weeded out a potential worm, so I'll let you come once your ass is red and stinging."

"Oh how kind of you. Let me bow at your feet in reverence of your greatness." I place my hands under my chin and bat my eyelashes at him sweetly—and also full of all the sarcasm in the world.

He shakes his head, that hint of a smile playing on his lips again.

"Penis chocolate, best idea ever. Please do it again next year," Lina says in my opposite ear. "Marco, we're keeping her. That guy was an asshole and kept leering at me all throughout dinner. He gave me the creeps, so I'm glad he's gone."

"Gone where? What happened to him?" I pop in a chocolate cock in my mouth and let it melt on my tongue. I'm expecting Lina to answer but it's Marco's voice that greets my ear.

"Let's just say it's difficult to disrespect someone when you're missing a tongue."

I choke on my melted chocolate, trying my best not to cause a scene as the fucker calmly taps my back like he hasn't just admitted to cutting some guy's tongue out.

Although, technically, he couldn't have done it since he's been here the whole time.

Enzo returns a few minutes later—no visible blood on his hands—and immediately disappears again, following Lina to wherever she's going. After our discussion earlier, she explained the whole bodyguard thing as something she could do without, but considering how hot Enzo is, she's coping... with orgasms that her brother must absolutely never find out about.

I jump in my seat at a sudden intrusion inside my panties and slowly turn my head to find Marco facing straight ahead as if nothing is going on underneath the table. He's observing the room, at least that's how it looks. After a few slides up and down my wet slit, he pulls his hand away, bringing it up to his mouth. That's when I notice one of the chocolates in his hand, glistening. Turning his head, his steel-gray eyes bore into mine and the smirk on his face makes me want to smack it off him and sit on it all at the same time. He slowly opens his mouth and places his plump lips around his own fingers, devouring the chocolate with one bite and sucking his fingers clean.

My chest is literally heaving at the filthy act and I want more.

"On that note…" Marco stands, tapping a small spoon against his Champagne glass to get everyone's attention again after the low rumbles of conversation started back up once Eric left. "Thank you, everyone, for joining us this evening at our annual Christmas Eve party. Any and all business will be concluded after the holidays, because as you know, the Mancini's believe in *famiglia*, and this is a time for us all to be with our loved ones. Speaking of, we have an addition to our famiglia this year. I'd like to introduce you all to my fiancé." He looks down at me, holding out his hand for me to stand with him. Fuck sake. I take it, standing as gracefully as I can with a mouth full of penis chocolate—Eric and his goons just left theirs behind, someone had to eat it. "I present to you, River Fox, soon to be River Mancini. She has earned my respect, my trust…" He pauses to bring my left hand to his mouth and kisses the knuckle just above my engagement ring. "And my love. I expect you to welcome her into our world like the queen she is about to become."

There's a round of applause as we sit down, like we're in a fucking theatre, and while I'm good with all the attention usually, I probably shouldn't have drunk as many of Stefano's amazing cocktails as I have. He just appears, as if by magic, every time my glass is empty. Drinking on the job has never been something I've really done—I like to keep a clear head—but with everything that's gone on with my life lately, I've let those walls down. My heart is surely locked up, while my inhibitions are running wild.

A song starts playing through the speakers, one I know well as it sits at the top of my most played on my Spotify. Gavin Mikhail's version of *Demons*. Not exactly what I thought would be played at this event, I expected all Christmas themed music, but color me surprised. I close my eyes and listen to the words and the beautiful piano.

"Dance with me, *Dolcezza*." It's not a question. I open my eyes as I'm pulled back to standing by Marco and he leads me to the area cleared for dancing.

"What if I don't wanna dance?" I challenge him, looking him in the eyes as he brings me into him, keeping one hand in mine at my chest, and the other grazing the top of my ass as I wrap my spare arm around his neck.

"Just enjoy the moment."

I want to bite back, but I really fucking love this song. It speaks to me on so many levels, which is the only reason I relent.

Pulling me onto the dance floor, he makes a big show of twirling me around before pulling me back into him.

Our clasped hands are pressed between our chests as his free hand rests possessively on the small of my back.

"I shouldn't be surprised that you're a good dancer, should I?" I mean, he's a control freak so obviously he's mastered the art of seduction on a dance floor.

"No, you shouldn't. I'm good at everything I do." My gaze darts up to his, ready to roll my eyes at his conceited attitude only to find a devilish grin on his beautiful lips. It's so rare and sincere that it knocks the air from my lungs with how sexy he looks.

"You're an ass." Spinning us around, he brings his mouth to my ear, his vanilla scent wafting around me, making my knees weak.

"Speaking of..." His pinky discreetly rubs just above the crack of my ass.

"For someone who smells like vanilla, you sure as hell have spicier tastes." I freeze at the sound of his laughter. It's the first time I've heard the deep rumble, and coupled with his head thrown back, his Adam's apple bobbing with every movement of his vocal chords, I'm completely and utterly mesmerized.

"Jesus, the things that come out of your mouth. And for your information, Lina and I were forced to take music and dance lessons." Our bodies resume the gentle swaying, the song nearing its end when he pulls me impossibly closer. "Besides, vanilla has a bad reputation. In fact, to create the scent, you need layers upon layers." We're staring at each other, contemplating the other's next move. I'm certain that from the vantage point of the guests in the room, all they see is two people deeply in love.

"Hmm, just like you?" Every day, I discover another thing about this man that intrigues me.

"No, *Dolcezza,* just like you."

Dancing with Marco is like having slow, sensual sex standing up. His breath against my neck, like barely-there kisses against my skin, the way his thumb presses against the top of my ass like a dark promise, the way his hold is tight and possessive, owning me, all the while letting me move freely...

For a few moments, I forget the world around me and just dance.

With a gentle tap on my ass, Marco spins me again before we head back to the table.

"Rose?"

Fuuuuck.

"Tyler? What are you doing here?"

Marco is schmoozing with some people at the next table over, and here in front of me is the one and only, Tyler fucking Walker.

"One of my companies is aligned with Mancini Hotels. Marco and I go way back."

Fuck. How could I forget where my referral to Marco came from?

"So, engaged, huh?" He doesn't look sad about it, which is good. I truly thought I'd broken the poor man's heart when I turned him down, but it seems I held more stock in myself than needed.

"Yup." I can't find any other words. This is awkward as fuck. I have no clue if Tyler knows about me having a contract in place with Marco, and I'm sure as shit not going to be the one to bring it up.

"Lina? Is that you?" Tyler zones in on Lina as she comes back to the table, Vincenzo right behind her—as he has been all evening whenever she moves.

"Ty! Oh my God! I haven't seen you for years. How are you?" Her eyes become wide as saucers as she drinks him in—I don't blame her, he is hot as fuck. I'm suddenly forgotten as Tyler's attention is all on Lina, and I can see the lust flying between them both, even as they pretend there's nothing there.

A hand wraps around my waist from behind, and the unmistakable scent of Marco surrounds me.

"Tyler." I feel him nod over my shoulder. "Eyes off my woman."

Tyler grins, throwing me a playful wink. "Don't worry, they're already elsewhere."

I know exactly where they are, but I'm saying nothing. Not my circus and all that.

"*Dolcezza*, let's go. I can't stand to watch you speak with other men any longer. Upstairs. Now." The last word is a low growl, one that has my pussy fluttering in anticipation of what's to come.

I wonder if he could beat Tyler's record? Maybe I'll have to try that one day. That's for another time though, right now, I could internally combust with all the not-sex I've been having lately and I smile seductively at the asshole with beautiful deep gray eyes.

"Sir, yes sir."

Chapter Thirteen
River

More often than not, when people say, "I'm going to New York," what they're really saying is "I'm going to Manhattan." It's crazy how such a small island has taken center stage across the world. With barely twenty-three square miles of land, this borough is the greatest destination in the hearts of tourists. All year round, they come and go with maps on their phones and awe on their faces.

I see them now, high up on my Fifth Avenue perch, as they walk around like ants hoping to catch sight of the rich and famous of the Upper East Side. Burrowed in their coats, they *ooh* and *aah* as they walk by, crossing the street and losing themselves in the lungs of The City.

"You look stunning in that dress." I don't startle as he speaks. The whole time I spent contemplating the world's love of New York City, I could feel his imposing presence behind me.

"You said that, thank you." Without turning around, I speak to the pristine window. Absently, I wonder how many times they're cleaned for them to look so perfect.

"You're upset." It's not a question, he can feel something stirring in me.

"Contemplative, I think. I miss my family and not going home for Winter Solstice feels weird." When I do turn around, he's right there, his gorgeous face mere inches from my lips.

"I've kept you from them. I'm sorry." One finger comes up and brushes a stray hair from my cheek, pushing it behind my ear. "It's in our contract."

It is. Seeing my family is non-negotiable.

"I hated seeing Tyler so close to you." His words are barely audible as he speaks softly in my ear. "And at the funeral, I had this uncontrollable urge to hurt Nate." My head tilts back as his mouth hovers just above my skin, down the column of my neck and over my collar bone.

"Why is that? He was just a client. And how *do* you know Nathaniel?" His hand is suddenly in my hair, pulling my head back with his eyes boring into mine.

"I'm just a client, too." His words are factual but his tone is all wrong.

"Yes." It doesn't escape me that my second question goes unanswered.

"Hmm..." Then his mouth is on mine. Lips searching out my lips. Tongue battling with my tongue. Breaths mingling with my breaths. Nothing about this kiss screams job or client. It's possessive and hungry. It's all-consuming with its urgency. His entire body is kissing me as he wraps his free hand over my exposed thigh and brings my leg up and around his waist. With fingers digging into my flesh and teeth biting into my lower lip, the simple act of pulling air into my lungs feels insurmountable. My body acts of its own volition, seeking out more of his heat, needing more of his touch.

"What do you want, River?" It takes me a minute to understand the question, not sure why he's even asking me. Fucking is part of the contract, this is a no-brainer.

"What?" My question is barely a word, just a mumbled sound spilling from between my lips.

His hand at my thigh slides over my hip and latches onto the silky fabric before pulling hard enough to rip, giving him better access to my ass.

"Dammit, I loved this dress." Why am I even thinking about that right now? My pussy is swollen with need, hungry for his touch, yet the only thing I can truly focus on is the fact that he just ruined an exquisite garment.

"Fuck the dress. Answer me."

"I don't..." Fingers run over the crack of my ass, sliding down until he reaches my very wet and needy pussy, pushing two fingers inside and holding me hostage to our lust. We both go still, our chests heaving to the beat of the passing seconds.

"What. Do. You. Want?" Punctuating his question with a bite to my bottom lip, he curls his fingers just enough to make me jolt in his arms.

"You. I want *you*." Our mouths crash together, teeth clashing and tongues searching for an explanation to this fire that's clearly burning inside of us both. It's different from Tyler. Yes, he was hot and he was fucking talented, but this feels more primal. More urgent.

Marco doesn't feel like a client, and that thought scares the ever-living shit out of me.

Our entire bodies shaking from our kiss, Marco steps back just enough to put much needed distance between us. I'm guessing he's afraid of what's going on, too—needing to get his wits about him.

"Strip. I want to see your cunt dripping with your cum. Show me how much you need me."

Or maybe not. Maybe this is par for his sexual course.

Shaking off the sudden jealousy at the thought that he could feel this kind of desire for any other woman, I straighten my shoulders and raise my chin, ready to put on my working mask.

His fingers are immediately at my jaw, his eyes burning with a fire Satan himself would covet.

"Don't do that. You do not hide from me, River. Not now, not ever. There is no Rose between us, do you understand?" I'm taken aback by his words. We barely know each other, how could he possibly see my change in attitude? Most days, not even Kai would notice.

With his eyes trained on me as he steps back again, I reach for the seam at my side and slide the hidden zipper down as far as it'll go. Without prompting, the satin falls down my body and pools at my feet like lava from a volcano. I'm hot and wet and thick with lust. Stepping out to avoid damaging it even further, I move closer to Marco, flicking the clasp at the front of my bra and tossing the lace aside.

Even in my heels, Marco towers over me like a skyscraper dominating the entire city. It's like I'm the lost tourist and he's the landmark that keeps me oriented.

Hooking my thumbs in the sides of my panties, I'm about to pull them down when Marco reaches over and stops my movement.

"Wait." I freeze, the rasp in his voice making my skin pebble with goosebumps.

Perfectly dressed in his tux, he takes my wrists in one hand and pins them at the small of my back. My breasts are full, my nipples rubbing against the soft fabric of his five-thousand-dollar Tom Ford tuxedo. Heat emanates from his body, warming my naked form as he takes me in, one frustrating inch at a time.

Then he's on his knees and this time I'm the one looking down on him, I'm the one towering over this bigger-than-life man who commands a room with a flick of his wrist and a scowl on his ridiculously handsome face.

A forefinger taps the inside of my thigh—a silent order to spread them—before he hooks it inside the crotch of my lace undies, pulling the fabric down but not letting me step out of them. My ankles are prisoners, just like my wrists are held hostage by his firm grip. My pussy is on display, his mouth just inches from where I need it.

Reaching up to my heavy tits, he engulfs one in his large hand and squeezes almost to the point of pain, except all I feel is delirious with wanting him. He flicks a nipple, causing me to cry out in surprise.

"You need a little pain with your pleasure, *Tesoro*. A little chaos with your control." Digging his nails into my skin, he rakes a slow and tortuous path down the middle of my stomach, killing me with the anticipation of his touch.

"Yes."

I can feel him pressing harder, probably leaving a trace that he was here, causing me to ache in the best of ways.

"Watch me while I feast on your cunt. All wet and dripping for me." I clench the walls of my pussy, earning a hum from Marco. "Dripping, indeed, *Tesoro*."

I don't expect his mouth on me, so when the first lick of his thick, hot tongue drags from back to front, my knees almost buckle from the relief. The pressure at my wrists is gone, but my instinct tells me not to move them, not to move anything while he fucks my pussy with his mouth.

I'm not naïve enough to think he's in a submissive pose. He may be the one on his knees but he's wielding all the power in this scenario and frankly, I need this. I need to lose the tight hold on everything going on.

With both of his hands on the globes of my ass, he pulls me into his mouth and kisses me like a long-lost lover. Licking and sucking and biting at any flesh he can touch. At this point, I'm riding his face, fucking him with the rocking of my pelvis, silently begging him to flick my clit so I can feel the imminent release.

Somehow, he knows. He can feel my orgasm approaching so he stops. I'm certain he does it on purpose.

Licking a trail from my clit to my navel to my chest and up the length of my throat, he attacks my mouth with the same heat he'd shown while eating my pussy. Voracious and urgent.

"Step out of your panties but keep your shoes on." I don't even hesitate. The lace is gone as I stand there, my fleeting patience making my skin buzz with need.

"On the bed and let your head hang off the side." A sly grin forms on my lips as I realize he's going to be the one fucking my mouth now. Finally, he's giving me more than just random orgasms. Finally, he's letting me touch him, allowing me to give him pleasure.

Finally... he's taking instead of only giving.

"Yes, Sir."

Walking me to the giant bed, the colors matching the masculine feel of the bedroom—all earthy and somber—with one hand at the base of my spine guiding me where he wants me, he glides his pinky finger down the crack of my ass and whispers, "Soon," like an omen.

I may talk a big game, but fucking my ass has never been on the table. Yet his warning feels more like a promise I don't want to resist.

I tell myself that it's my job.

I tell myself that it's in the contract.

I tell myself that he's just another client.

I lie to myself as the slickness between my pussy lips travels down my inner thighs.

Two fingers pinch my bottom lip, his grip tight, almost uncomfortable as he leans impossibly closer.

"This mouth," his tongue sweeps across my lip then his mouth is on mine again. Demanding entrance, exuding control. "I never know whether I want to punish it or fuck it."

I'm hoping for both.

Ignoring the errant thought that has no place in this work environment, I focus instead on the feel of his heated touch, the glide of his wet tongue. The pinch of his punishing fingers. The pain and the pleasure so intimately linked that I don't know where one ends and the other begins.

Severing our link, he pushes me down onto the mattress and positions himself at the foot of the bed as I hang my head upside down as instructed. From this angle, he looks larger than life. Bigger than the universe itself.

He looks every bit the dangerous man I expect him to be.

"Unzip me." I blink as my brain tries to visualize the mechanics while everything is upside down. Slowly, I reach over and do as he asks. More like orders, but I'll let it slide if it means I get to finally see him naked.

I'm beginning to understand that teasing me is his favorite game as he pops open every single button, painstakingly slow. I'm not above begging, but I'm afraid if I say anything it'll sound like an order and then he'll just walk away since, apparently, his self-control is gargantuan.

Once he's done, he throws his shirt to the side without a single care that it's worth more than some people's monthly incomes. All thoughts of clothing go out the window when ridges of his sculpted chest and abs come into view. Even in this position, I can see that he's built like a Greek god and just as hard as their statues.

Tweaking my nipple, he reaches over me, rubbing his barely-covered crotch across my face as he grabs my thighs and folds my legs over so he's using my shoe-clad feet as leverage. Fucking hell, I'll be feeling those muscles in the morning.

"Pull my slacks down." Taking in a deep breath, I inhale his unique spice with a touch of vanilla, letting it soothe me like a balm after a burn. I do as I'm told and when his cock pops out, it's all I can see. All I can smell. Earthy and sweet like he was born from the freshly labored soil.

"Open up, Tesoro. Swallow me whole." Opening my mouth—my tongue out and waiting—I breathe through my nose as he presses down on my ankles and slowly pushes his hips forward. Inch by delicious inch, I take him in until I feel the tip of his head nudging the back of my throat.

"That's it, take it deep. Suck hard, Tesoro." I'm eager to show him how much I want this, want him. But he takes me by surprise as he pushes all the way in and leans forward just enough to lick a hot path over my clit and between my swollen lips.

My gasp is silent but his moan tells me he felt it vibrating on his cock. Pulling all the way out, I take advantage of the moment to lick him up and around before he pushes back inside, this time with less elegance and more force. Once again, when he's bent over me, his dick pushing into my throat without a single fuck to give, he tortures me with that talented tongue of his.

This time, he licks me twice and I groan against his hard length, and I swear to fuck he trembles at the feel of it.

"Fuck, Tesoro. Do that again." I don't need prompting, since he's the one making me react every time he teases my sensitive and needy clit.

My moan is almost one of pain as he flicks my bundle of nerves then bites one of my lips before standing back up and fucking my mouth once, twice, and a third time, making me gag hard enough to make my eyes water.

His thumbs come to the corners of my eyes and wipe off my tears.

"Do you know what's more beautiful than you sucking hard on my dick?"

I shake my head because this is not the time for riddles.

"Seeing you cry while you're sucking hard on my dick. It's poetic. Erotic. And it's about to make me come."

All hell breaks loose as he slams into my mouth once more and latches his mouth onto my clit until I fall completely apart. I'm gasping and choking with his dick buried in my throat, almost ready to tap out a safe word when my orgasm comes out of nowhere, hitting me straight at the bottom of my stomach and traveling through my bloodstream, making me silently scream around his cock.

Before I can even come down from the intensity of the moment, he spins me around so that my head is at the headboard, my knees practically falling onto the bed from my lack of muscle control. Grabbing onto my wrists, he traps them in one of his hands while the other presses firmly on my thigh as he slams inside my pussy and stills.

"Fuck, River. I've waited so fucking long for this moment." I'm heaving, my breaths are shallow and my heartbeat is a steady staccato as he digs his fingertips into my leg, burying himself to the hilt.

"Why? Why have you waited? You're pa—" His mouth slams against mine, kissing my words away. Stealing my phrase so it doesn't echo into the universe.

Then he fucks me like I'm his saving grace or his much-needed release. Thrusting in and out with abandon, he steals my breath and my gasps. He swallows my pleasure as I come apart once again before I feel him freeze, his cum coating my walls as he holds our kiss.

Releasing my mouth, he peppers kisses across my cheek down to my ear as he whispers, "Because it's not about me. It's only about what you need."

Chapter Fourteen
River

I'm angry.

At Marco. At myself. At this whole ridiculous situation.

There's a reason Escorts don't agree to marriage with their clients, and I'm certain the only reason I said yes is because of all the shit that's been thrown my way recently. My mind is all over the place, and I'm clearly not making good decisions anymore.

I had my shit together, life was good. The weird phone calls and texts were merely an annoyance I could have done without, but *sticks and stones* and all that. Speaking of, I can't remember the last time I received one of those calls. Since beginning my contract with Marco, it all seems to have stopped, and I'm not sure if that's comforting or concerning.

Admittedly, having my skin sliced off, receiving a dick in a box, being attacked in an alley, and watching one of my best friends die have all been fucking awful and shitty things—fuck, I'm really racking up the traumas this year. It's no wonder I'm not exactly in the best headspace. I keep pushing it all aside, almost pretending it hasn't happened to me, it happened to someone else. It happened to River. River isn't as strong as Rose. Rose has a job to do, a life to make for her family.

I know my big picture, but I find focusing on smaller things each day is how I do this without going insane thinking about all the shit, what happened with Nathaniel... and Kai.

While I'll do whatever it takes to make my family happy, that doesn't mean I can't be angry with life right now. The main thing I'm focusing on today—as I have been the last few days since Christmas Eve—is that I'm pissed at Marco for not using a fucking condom. Yes, I have the shot, the sex was amazing, and I've never come so hard in all my life, but, that's not the fucking point.

Yesterday, I had the contract out, ready to show Marco that he broke his side of the deal because I always include a condom clause... but could I find it? Fuck no. I have been through the contract with a fine-tooth comb, and it isn't there. The fucker must have done his stupid voodoo and removed it—or *his guy* did—and there's no way I can prove it was there because it's even gone from the hard-copy, with my signature right on the dotted line.

Doesn't mean I'll be letting him go bareback again though. Fucking asshole.

With a deep breath, I smooth my hands over my jeans before grabbing the handle of my suitcase and prepare to leave my bedroom—I've been relegated back to this room instead of Marco's after refusing sex without a condom. He's been refusing me orgasms as retaliation, and after three days of having his mouth and tongue on my pussy, without the big O, all I want to do is punch him in the dick.

"You won't be needing that suitcase today, *Dolcezza*." Marco barges into my room, lucky I wasn't closer to the door as he came in, or that shit would've knocked me out.

"The fuck I will. I'm going to my brother's for a couple days. It's in the contract." Resting my hands on my hips, in what I'm hoping looks like a power pose, I raise my eyes in expectancy. Just waiting for him to refuse me, because in his words, *Marco Mancini does not break a contract.*

"It is, *Dolcezza*. The contract states that you will be allowed to see your brother, Everest, and his wife, Petal, for at least two days in between Christmas and New Year for Yule activities." One corner of his lips lift, a cocksure smirk on his annoyingly beautiful face.

"Right, so I'm going now. We agreed today worked." I'm not backing down. These next few days are mine, especially considering Marco wants to get married on New Year's Eve.

"*Dolcezza*, come. Stop being stubborn." He holds his hand out for me, and because I'm curious more than anything, I take it with a roll of my eyes.

Leaning down so he's at my eye level, his smirk turns devilish, the corners of his eyes crinkling with mischief. "I'm going to spank your ass for every eye roll on our wedding night, *Dolcezza*. Start counting."

"Fuck off."

Before I realize what's happening, Marco has me against the wall, my arms pinned above my head with one of his gigantic hands. His other is unbuttoning my jeans and quickly making its way into my panties.

"What the fuck are you doing, Marco?"

I'm his not-so-unwilling prisoner as he thrusts two thick fingers inside me.

"What did I say about cursing?"

Curling his fingers, he has me in every way right now, pushing in and out roughly, his palm grazing my clit. I feel my nipples pebble against my bra, and through all the material, they still rub against Marco's hard, shirt-covered chest, causing a building tsunami in my underwear.

Before I can answer him, he thrusts in again, pausing there and bringing his mouth down to my mine, his breath tickling over my skin. "This mouth is too pretty for profanity. I can find much better uses for it." His tongue darts out and licks the seam of my lips before he nips at me and begins devouring me completely. Kissing me with abandon, tasting every inch of me as he continues to fuck me with his fingers, and just as the building pressure feels like it can't build any more, he fucking stops.

"Who does this cunt belong to?" He speaks after nipping at my tongue, then licks it better as he waits for an answer I don't want to give him.

"Me. It belongs to me," I bite back. He won't let me orgasm anyway, he's been withholding it the last few days... what's a few more? I can finish myself off in bed like I have been whenever I'm alone. It's not the same, but it'll do—I feel like a horny fucking teenager with the number of times I've masturbated lately.

Slowly pulling out of me, he grins, and pushes back inside, his palm hitting just right and making me groan. "I said, who does this cunt belong to, Tesoro?" He begins sliding his hand backward and forward, in and out, rubbing against all the spots that make my legs shake.

Groaning again, I look him square in the eye. "Me." My voice is breathy, and even I don't believe what I'm saying, because right now, this man is owning my pussy like a fucking champion.

He chuckles, a deep, grumbly kind that makes my nipples impossibly harder.

"One more time. Who does this cunt belong to?" Bending his head, one hand still holding my arms up, the other inside my panties, he bites through my top in exactly the right place to get my nipple.

"Oh God, Marco." The sensations running through my body keep building and I swear I'm going to pass out as he starts flicking my nipple with his tongue, the damp material from his spit adding to the sensations.

"That wasn't so difficult, was it?" His thrusts become faster, deeper, his need for my nipple more urgent as he drops my arms and lifts my top to remove the barrier between his mouth and my skin. He sucks, and flicks, and bites down, and every nerve ending is on fire, my breathing erratic as I run my fingers through his hair, pulling at it as an orgasm rips through my body and I scream at the sensations.

Definitely not the same as doing it myself.

"There's my good girl," he says at my ear.

Coming down from the best orgasm since Christmas Eve, I realize the fucker thinks I was answering his question, when it was just a slip of the tongue. His name only left my lips in a moment of weak passion. My cunt does not belong to him.

"Get off me. I have a ferry to catch, and all you're doing is holding me up." I push at his solid chest, and he slides his fingers from my panties, causing me to shudder as he grazes over my slit.

"Mmm, you taste so sweet, *Dolcezza*. But know, the next time you come will be on my bare dick, after you've begged me to fuck you."

Resting his fingers against my mouth, he forces my lips open and pushes inside. I want to bite down, but instead, I roll my eyes and suck, like the good girl I absolutely am not.

"That's two, *Dolcezza*." His fingers leave my mouth with a pop of my lips from the suction, and he immediately puts them in his own mouth, sucking them clean with his eyes closed in some kind of freaky ecstasy as he moans.

"Whatever, Marco. I need to leave."

With eyes now open again, he grabs my chin and forces my gaze to meet his. "Downstairs. Now."

"Fine, but then I have to go." I roll my shoulders back in defiance and angrily sort my clothes out so I don't look like I've just been finger-fucked against a wall.

Halfway down the stairs with Marco, I hear voices... voices I recognize, and I pause. Did he really...?

"You're a controlling dick. Very clever, asshole," I whisper so quietly, but he hears me before I remove my hand from his and continue down the stairs, Marco following close behind.

"It kinda gives me the creeps, there's just something here that shouldn't be and it's throwing the whole house off."

"It's a fucking monstrosity is what it is."

I move my feet faster, my face hurting from the grin I can't help but give my brother and sister-in-law before I pull them both in for a hug. Carefully, of course, because Ev's still on crutches with his leg plastered up.

"River!" They both sing-song in unison, wrapping their arms around me in the most awkward three-way hug known to man.

"Hey, beautiful." Petal winks at me as we part, rubbing her hand up and down my arm in that wonderful, soothing way she does.

"Hey, gorgeous." I peck her on the cheek before giving her one last squeeze. I'm still beaming as I ask, "What are you guys doing here?"

"This dude behind you arranged everything. I'll be honest, Riv, this is all a little weird." Ev doesn't look too impressed, but Petal has a whimsical look on her face.

"When Marco came to visit, he explained the connection you both share, and how much he freaking loves you. Then he asked Ev for your hand in marriage, and, babe, his aura said it all. There's no way we could have said no." She squeals and hugs me again, squeezing tightly.

Turning to look at Marco, I raise an eyebrow. He visited them? He actually stepped foot on Staten Island? I'm gob-smacked. How he ever got Petal and Ev on his side, I'll never know. He's clearly been telling some untruths, but Petal's read on people is hardly ever wrong. Though, I'm not sure why I'm surprised. It's like Marco Mancini was born under a lucky star. He shrugs his shoulders and smiles.

"Have fun with your family, *Dolcezza*. Stefano will show them to their room and then the next few days are yours.

I've arranged a car to take you shopping in fifteen minutes." He turns to address Ev next. "Ensure the girls get whatever their hearts desire. It's all on me."

"I have my own money, Marco." I glare at him.

"I know, but this is for our wedding. Allow me."

"What?"

"You need a dress for Saturday. Your bridesmaids also need dresses. So go, shop."

Bridesmaids? Plural? I'm about to question him when Lina comes bouncing down the stairs in all her glamorous glory. Her hair is tied back into a slick ponytail, and even in jeans and a t-shirt, she looks like she could walk the runway.

"Oh my God, you must be Petal! Words do you no justice. You're beautiful. Is it okay if I hug you?"

The smile that crosses Petal's face is infectious. It almost makes me sad that Lina isn't going to be a permanent friend.

"Er, duh. Come here, gorgeous!"

They both squeeze as tightly as the other. As they separate, Petal does her thing, holding Lina by the arms and really looking at her. Lina doesn't flinch, she just accepts what's happening.

"So much light." Petal's eyes flick over Lina's shoulder at Marco, ever-so-briefly but I see it, and she smirks as she stares into Lina's soul. "Sometimes secrets are okay." Winking, Petal lets go of her and settles into Ev's side. He can't hold her like he usually does, as he's holding crutches, but he kisses the top of her head with a serene smile anyway.

"Your car is here, Miss Fox." Stefano appears out of nowhere, as usual, holding the front door open for us.

"I've told you to call me River, none of that Miss Fox business. Keep Mr. Grumps out of trouble." I laugh as I give Stefano a shoulder nudge before being pulled back by my wrist.

Marco spins me to face him and takes my face in his hand, bringing my head closer to his so he can devour my mouth like a starving man.

"Dude, that's my sister."

"Oh, look at how sweet they are."

"Gross, that's my brother."

They all speak at once as Marco pulls away, kissing my forehead before turning me again and spanking my ass as I walk out.

"Have fun, *Dolcezza*."

We have been shopping for hours, but I won't complain too much. The staff in this shop have been very attentive. One of them even went out to a local vegan place to make sure Petal and Ev had snacks. Marco booked the appointment in this wedding dress store on Madison Avenue, and I have a sneaky feeling he's made it worth their while for just hosting us. This amount of attention isn't normal, and nobody else has been in to shop.

Petal and Lina have found their dresses, and I've tried on two floofy things that make me look like I belong in fairy land. All I asked of the girls was that they chose something that made them feel beautiful. I'm not all about the matchy-matchy, and considering this wedding is a whole big farce anyway, they might as well have new dresses that they like.

Petal's is all black, but with a rainbow petticoat that flares out like a tutu underneath the short skirt. The top half is corseted with long, black-lace sleeves, with accents of shiny rainbow-colored crystals throughout. It's perfect, and her eyes nearly popped out of her head when she saw it. She took some persuading, insisting she would be able to find something in a local thrift store rather than contributing to a big chain, but when she found out the shop we're in is family-run, she conceded.

Lina's dress fits her curves like a glove, the deep blue satin hitting her in all the right places as it falls around her hips to her feet. It's sleeveless, but she's chosen a matching blue chiffon wrap to wear with it, mainly so she's covered up while her parents are there, then she can remove it when they're gone.

Ev has been so patient with us all, sitting on the couch opposite the changing rooms and giving encouragement with each new gown. His eyes nearly bugged out of his head when he saw Petal in her first outfit, it was so tight it looked painted on.

Now that the girls have their dresses, I have no more excuses to avoid finding mine. The two I've tried on were mainly for shits and giggles. I may be marrying Marco for a contract, for money, but that doesn't mean I don't want to look and feel like the queen I'm pretending to be.

"Miss Fox, I have a dress your fiancé has chosen for you in the changing room. Please follow me." The main lady that's been helping us, Julia, must be in her fifties, and she told us she's been working here for thirty years. It's clear she loves her job, the smiles she gives with each new dress on a body are always real.

"Okay." I turn to address the others, "I've got one to try, get ready to cry your asses off with how beautiful I'm about to look when I come out."

With a thumbs up from Ev, and excited claps and mini squeals from the girls, I follow Julia into the changing area, skeptical about what Marco has *chosen* for me. Because of course he fucking has. I might just get one of the floofy ones to piss him off.

"You know the drill now, darling. Into your undies, please."

After stripping down, I wait in anticipation for what I'm about to see behind the zipped bag. Wait, does that mean he's already bought it?

"Close your eyes. I'm going to dress you, and then you can open them and get the full effect."

Again, I do as she asks, holding my arms in the air, and a really soft material slides down over my body. The feel of ribbons being tightened and tied at my back makes me believe I at least have a corset over my top half, and the material on my legs feels like it stops at my knees. She does something with my hair, then something cold touches my neck.

"Okay, all done." She moves me forward a few steps so I'm in front of the mirror. "Open your eyes, darling."

I could actually cry. I was all set to hate this dress, ready to say no and choose something for myself. But wow, this dress is spectacular. The material is all white silk, with clear crystals all over the skirt that flows out from my knees into a small train. The top is ruched in such a way that makes all my curves look a little extra, and it's so simple and understated, yet magnificent in every way. There's even a headpiece. A shoulder-length veil adorned in crystals with a pretty lace edge, and a crystal headband keeping it in place.

"That's the one, isn't it? It's very rare a man can choose a woman's dress. Your fiancé must really love you, darling. You're a lucky lady indeed."

I just nod and smile. No point in letting the poor lady know the truth and ruining her day.

"Let's go and show your family, shall we?"

Following her through the curtain, she leads me to the little plinth in front of the couches and instructs me to stand on it before moving my skirt so it flares out just right.

Ev, Petal, and Lina are all wide-eyed, and the girls cover their mouths. They're the polar opposites of each other in terms of lifestyle and belief, but their personalities are creepily similar.

"Sis, wow. Mom and Dad would be so proud." Ev struggles to stand, and I tell him to stop as tears fill my eyes, but he doesn't listen. Instead, Petal helps him, and he hobbles over to me on his crutches. I bend to hug my little brother, squeezing my eyes closed to stop the tears.

Lina is next in line, waiting to give me a hug.

"River, you look stunning. My brother is a very lucky man."

Then it's Petal's turn, but she doesn't embrace me like I'd expect. Instead, she takes my hand and leads me back into the changing room.

"Everything okay, Pet?"

"Of course it is, silly. Look, you know we all love you, but just a couple months ago, we were being introduced to Nathaniel, you're still pining over Kai, and now you're about to marry someone else. Are you sure this is what you want? Your aura isn't as bright as usual, it's almost like something's unraveling. This all feels wrong somehow. You're supposed to get married in March." That's when she does hug me, and holds me like only Petal can. "You have found your soulmate, I can see it. Your soul recognizes it, but you're afraid and you feel unworthy. Babe, you're a goddess, please allow yourself to believe it."

"Is this your pep talk? Because I'll be honest, it's not my favorite."

"Well, I think you need it. Because we love you, and if you're just doing this because you're in the same situation as Freya, you know we'll never judge you."

"I can promise you, this is not the same thing."

"Good. But make sure you come and visit us soon. Or at least charge up your crystals and meditate once in a while."

"Thanks for looking out, Pet. I love you."

"Love you too. Now let's get you out of this beautiful dress so we can go and enjoy that rooftop garden you were telling us about."

CHAPTER FIFTEEN
RIVER

Yule was simple this year. Petal brought the candles and incense, along with a deck of tarot cards, and Everest was the weed master. Lina left early, presumably for her bed, but I have doubts. As for me, well, I had nothing but my good intentions and need for family. It's when the doorbell rings, and Stefano whispers in my ear that I have two more guests, that things get interesting.

And by interesting, I mean awkward as fuck.

"Wow, River, you're moving up in the world. And here I thought Tyler Walker was the top of the money pile." I think I smile, but I'm pretty sure it's closer to a snarl.

"Freya, that's enough." Kai's words are a growl that instantly shut her mouth.

"Welcome to the Mancini home, come on in." What the fuck am I doing? It's like Marco is pulling the strings to this make-believe show and I'm just the puppet that recites the script.

A whistle echoes throughout the entry hall, bouncing off the four walls before spearing my stomach where anxiety resides.

"Oh, good! We're all here. Come on, let's celebrate the rebirth of a new year." Petal takes my hand and leads me to the corner of the living room where she has set up a makeshift altar and a circle of rosemary scented candles.

"River, hon, stand right here. Before we begin, you need to walk the path of the Earth. Be one with the cycle of life." Fuck, Petal really thinks I might be pregnant. Which isn't much of a stretch when you examine my life the last few months. And what am I going to say at our Spring celebration when this entire farce will be over? *Oops, false alarm?*

Bare feet join me at the candles as I step inside their lighted circle and begin walking around slowly, pausing at three, six, nine, and twelve like I'm the big hand of a large clock. The more I walk around, the more aligned I feel with the universe and time itself. With the pattern of the seasons. My body releases the stress of the last few weeks and it's empowering, this knowledge that I'm part of a greater force. That I'm not the puppet, I'm the master. I am time, I am nature itself.

I am River Fox and I know exactly where I stand in this universe.

"There she is," Petal murmurs to the room. "I've missed that aura." I can feel it, too. The blue waves of my existence surrounding me and welcoming me home.

After everyone has taken their turn, we head upstairs to the roof terrace. Stefano went ahead and lit the outdoor heaters for us so we could sit in the comfortable lounge chairs without freezing to death while we share a joint... or four.

"Okay, now that I'm high, I need some explanation, sister mine." Fuck. I haven't smoked in a while and I'm afraid I'll become a blabber mouth at this point.

"Well, brother mine, we are in The City. The Upper East Side," I say the words with a posh accent like I'm some British butler dismissing a mere mortal begging for change. "It's Yule and we're high as fuck." That pretty much sums up the whole scenario.

"Funny. I'm talking about your... men." Plural. Not Marco, but the entire menu of my private and professional lives.

"If I didn't know better, I'd think she's an escort." I choke at Freya's words, coughing like a newbie with her first toke.

"Easy, River. You okay?" Petal is my favorite human.

"Did you just call me a prostitute?"

"No, silly, I'm just saying... in the last few weeks, you've been... busy." Fucking Freya and her lack of filter.

"Freya, enough. What the fuck is your problem?" I should feel relief that Kai is defending me, but all I feel is annoyed.

"My problem? Your ex is making her way through the upper crust of New York's Forbes list and you're questioning *me*?" I have to remind myself that it's Yule and punching a bitch goes against my principles of leaving the past behind and embracing the future.

With that thought, the bickering between what are supposed to be lovebirds about to get married fades away and all I can hear is the clarity of my future.

The complexity of my feelings for Kai and how they are tied to my childhood more than my adulthood.

The reality that Nathaniel scares me because he's real and of all the men I've had in my life, he's never disappointed me. Freud would have a field day with that one. The scared little girl who was just a few months shy of being a legal adult has abandonment issues after her father dies right in front of her eyes.

After both her parents bled out while she sat in the back seat in shock. It took me almost five minutes to snap out of it and grab the phone to call 911.

Five minutes. That's how quickly my entire life went from normal to horrendous.

Suddenly, this job feels right. Marco as my client feels aligned with what the universe has in store for me, like I'm on the right path. I can see it all so effortlessly, like a movie reel right in front of my eyes.

"I should get married here, on this rooftop."

"Yes! Oh, yes, that's perfect. The energy here is invigorating and fresh. It's new beginnings." I smile at Petal because she gets it.

"One problem, though. Your wedding is in five days, isn't everything already planned?" I look at Everest and grin like a madwoman.

"What's the point of having all this money if you can't put it to good use?"

So maybe Everest was right. Changing the venue of a wedding isn't as easy as snapping fingers, but when Marco Mancini is your betrothed, shit gets done nonetheless. It's impressive, really. Like people are actually afraid for their lives if they say no to him.

But here I am, at the entrance to the rooftop, just mere days after my epiphany, waiting for the doors to open and for the path to lead me to my very-soon-to-be husband.

And to five million dollars.

The thought makes my stomach churn a little, making me instantly regret the shot of whisky that I took to calm my nerves.

Everest was supposed to walk me down the aisle but he's still on crutches. That's not how I ever dreamed of my wedding day, being led by my hopping brother.

Worse even, not once in my little girl dreams did I picture Kai walking me down the aisle. He was always supposed to be waiting for me at the altar.

Yet, here we are.

"This is ridiculous, Riv. Just say the word and I'll rescue you. I'll be the getaway driver." I smile at that, it's not like the thought hasn't crossed my mind. But every time it does, it feels wrong.

We're alone here, behind the closed doors waiting for the string quartet—yes, that's right, a fucking foursome with violins—to begin Vivaldi's second movement of *Winter Season*. Petal suggested it when she called me two days after our Yule. She said it was like sitting by the fire after a snowstorm.

In that slight window between life as I know it and life after, I turn to Kai and take advantage of the privacy we never seem to truly have.

"Why are you marrying Freya?" I'm surprised that the pang I usually get at the bottom of my stomach is lesser, almost gone.

"That's a hell of a question, Psyche. And we need to talk about that. But now isn't the right time. All I can say is she needs me." His honesty is refreshing, but his evasive answer only brings on more questions.

"You can't call me that anymore, Kai. Is she pregnant?" I mean, we are the last people to ever judge having children out of wedlock. Those ideas are purely religious. We don't abide by those rules.

"No, River. It would be so much simpler if she were." He bends and kisses my forehead as he whispers. "It's her story to tell, but know this," he holds my face with his big hands, his eyes watering from unshed tears. "In every one of my dreams, I was the one waiting for you at the altar." I smile, the lie of this day weighing down on me.

"Mine, too. I guess the universe had other ideas." We smile at each other and turn toward the doors as the first bow slides across the strings and prompts the doors to open onto a winter wonderland.

Petal and Lina insisted on surprising me and holy fuck, am I ever.

Our biggest problem when changing the venue was the fact that Marco and his family are Catholics, and although I'm willing to bet he hasn't been to church in years, it is expected of him to hold a traditional ceremony.

I, on the other hand, believe in no god at all.

Somehow, the scene in front of me is the marriage of both sides of the coin.

We step onto a white silk runner that matches my dress perfectly, along with the sashes at the backs of each—two rows of three chairs—all attributed to a person standing and holding a plush rolled up blanket to fight the chill. That was Everest's idea, a way to stave off the cold while we took our vows. The path is lined by leafless trees decorated with white paper roses and silk sashes blowing in the wind. Thankfully, the heaters are strategically placed or else we'd all freeze to death.

My gaze follows the center aisle all the way to the back, the violins seem louder, somehow, like they're goading me, telling me to concentrate on every detail. Urging me to look up and see what's waiting for me.

No, not what.

Who.

As soon as I look up, our eyes lock and everything else around me disappears. The people, the music, the feel of Kai's hand on mine as my fingers tighten around the crook of his elbow. I know we're walking because Marco is getting closer and closer, his attention solely on me, his expression stoic, his jaw tense and aware of every move, every breath I take.

The only visible emotion on his face comes from the flare of his nose as he seems to reel in every ounce of control.

I almost smile at that. The idea of him being unable to dominate anything, including emotions, seems preposterous. People I don't know whisper things in Italian, like they're blessing our union. Or cursing it. How the hell would I know the difference?

"We're almost there, Riv. Say the word."

I don't look at Kai, severing the link with Marco seems impossible. Running *is* impossible. Backing out feels cowardly. I give him a barely perceptible shake of my head but Marco sees it and, as if he can sense Kai's words, his gaze abandons me to land on the man standing next to me.

Nathaniel was protective of me when it came to Kai.

Marco? He looks like he wants to rip him limb from limb. I roll my eyes and, like a bone to a dog, I get Marco's attention right back on me.

"Four." His whispered threat makes me instantly wet. *Fucker.*

"He looks abusive, Riv. Jesus fucking Christ, how do you choose these thugs?"

This time I do turn to him and grin like he's my favorite person.

"I don't know, Kai? Have you looked in the mirror lately?" He snorts, and just like that, I'm turning back to Marco as Kai stops us at the altar, turns me, and kisses me on the forehead in some kind of broken-hearted goodbye.

Next to me, Marco's growls says more than any vocalized threat.

"Take care of yourself." Kai's last words bring unshed tears to my eyes. I want to scream that it's all fake, that it'll all be over soon—in three months—but I don't.

I play my role as I turn to Marco and he takes my hand from Kai's, ignoring him completely, and brings the back of my palm to his mouth with a kiss that melts my stubborn heart.

"I will erase every single touch of his from your body tonight, *Dolcezza*. And then some."

With those words, this wedding party needs to move the fuck on so I can get my punishments. And my orgasms.

An hour later, after I promised to love and cherish and blah blah blah, at the foot a bronze cross—how the fuck did they even get that monstrosity up here?—we are sitting at the dais of the wedding party table while everyone chats on and on, and Marco's hand is right back where it always is when we sit together. His parents are as lovely as the first time I met them, if not a little intimidating. His father, Alberto, doesn't say much, but he sees it all. He watches everything around him, guards protect him at every turn—two stand behind him always—as he assesses me every now and again. We danced once and he asked me what loyalty meant to me.

It was all very Godfatherly. Yet, a little sweet, too. In a fucked up crime family way.

His mother, Gabriella, is the original mold for Lina, without a doubt. A little less naïve though, for sure.

On my thigh, one thumb teases my skin like the devil on a good girl's shoulder.

A light tap on my shoulder pulls me back from the intensity of Marco's touch. When I turn, Kai is towering over me, his expression solemn with a hint of pain in his honey-colored eyes.

Marco's grip on my thigh intensifies almost to the point of pain and I realize he's reeling in his possessiveness just long enough to find out what Kai wants with me.

"Hey." Kai's eyes dart from me to Marco and back to me. "Ev's not feeling too well. His leg's throbbing so we're gonna head out, if that's okay?"

Marco's grip relaxes as he snaps his fingers in the air. Immediately, Stefano is at his side.

"Have the car take River's family home or wherever they need." I smile at his efficiency. There's something about a man who takes action.

Taking Kai's hand in mine, I squeeze and rise to my feet despite Marco's vice grip trying to hold me down. With one deadly scowl his way, my husband gives me a devil's grin that promises a whole lot of hurt with my pleasure as he releases me.

"I'll walk you all out."

I can feel Marco's gaze boring into my back, watching every one of my steps as I walk away. It's like he's taking this whole marriage thing seriously.

"I'm sorry, sis, but my leg is killing me right now. Do you mind if we head out? I need a joint to ease the pain." Bending at the waist, I give my little brother a huge hug.

I hate that he's leaving but his health is more important than this charade.

"Of course, Ev. I mean, it's over anyway. We'll probably just have some Champagne and call it a night." Petal throws her arms around me and squeezes with all her dainty might.

"I can't believe you're married." Lowering her voice just for me, she adds, "And before Kai."

"I heard that." Kai's rumble is surprisingly close, making me jump just a little.

"Good." Wow, Petal's throwing punches tonight. Must be the alcohol. Or maybe it's the exposure to so much money. It makes her grumpy.

After walking them out, I head back to my table and take my seat next to my husband, where his hand returns to its original position on my thigh. It's like he constantly needs to touch me.

"It's time." Vincenzo's voice rings out and all chatter ends immediately. The men stand at once, a choreography I don't necessarily understand.

"What's going on? Is everyone leaving?" Looking up at Marco, his smile is sincere, almost giddy, as he places his lips at the corner of my mouth.

"It's time, *Dolcezza*. My time." He stares at me for longer than is decent as every pair of eyes watches us. "No. Not mine, *our* time." As he towers over me, I'm even more confused now than I was seconds ago.

"The rite will begin." Alberto speaks, and the space has a balm of reverence that falls on it. "I, Alberto Guiseppe Mancini, of sound mind and pure heart, step down from the responsibility bestowed upon me by my ancestors and God."

Marco pulls me up so we are both standing as Vincenzo hands us each a white cloth. I have no idea what is happening, this whole scene was never a point of discussion between us and I'm sure everyone in attendance can see right through me.

"Marco Adriano Mancini, of sound mind and pure heart, do you accept your fate by stepping up to the throne bestowed upon you by your father and ancestors before him?" My new father-in-law sounds like a cult leader. I'm half expecting someone to be sacrificed right there on the dance floor.

I gasp when Enzo pulls out a knife and hands it to Marco.

I'm too stunned to speak, let alone move, as images of a lamb being flayed from ear to ear invade my mind.

"Please don't kill an animal. I can't..." Marco's eyes are laughing, like he finds my accusation cute.

"No one is dying tonight, *Dolcezza*." The grin that follows is pure evil. "Not yet."

"I do." Marco takes the knife and lifts his left hand, placing the blade at the base of his forefinger and pushing through diagonally, causing a gash that is soon overflowing with blood.

"Oh my God, Marco. What...?"

Then he grabs my left hand and before I can react or scream or knee him in the balls, his blade is slicing my palm from the base of my thumb diagonally to my pinky finger. So quickly, I don't have time to feel the pain, he joins our hands and our gashes are perfectly lined up.

"My blood is forever bound to your blood. As I am the son of Alberto Giuseppe Mancini, I will protect you and our destiny, from tonight until forever. By the power of my ancestors, I do swear." Vicenzo wraps both cloths around our joined hands, squeezes, and bows his head at us.

"Capo. Regina."

Everyone in attendance lines up like they're about to receive the blood of Christ, mimicking Enzo's moves. They come, they hold our cloth covered hands, then bow.

"Capo. Regina." Then turn to give way to the next person.

I think I'm in shock. Pretty damn sure this is all a fucking dream. Or better yet, a nightmare. Did he say from tonight until forever? That does not sound like three months to me.

Finally, when the line ends, Lina and her mother come to us and bow their heads. "*Figlio mio, mio Capo.*" Gabriella then turns to me and smiles. "You are family now, River. Your needs are our needs and your fears are ours to destroy. Your joys are ours to share. Welcome, Regina." What the actual fucking fuck?

I should be pulling away, telling Marco he can go right off and fuck himself with his bloodied palm, but again, the shock is keeping me frozen in place.

The last to stand in front of us is Alberto, repeating Gabriella's words. He turns to me as he places both of his hands on my cheeks and kisses one then the other. Like the motherfucking Godfather.

Is that what Marco just became? Is he the Marlon Brando of the Upper East Side? Holy shit, am I the wife of the head of a fucking criminal organization? I thought he owned hotels and maybe—*maybe*—dabbled in some shady shit, but this? Fuck my life.

Marco then turns to me, raises our joined hands as his other hand palms the back of my head, bringing me in for a scorching kiss that, despite this very what-the-fuck moment, has my toes curling in my crystal Jimmy Choo's.

The shock is slowly wearing off when he releases me, a little tug of my lower lip with his teeth, my hard stare telling him very clearly and without negotiation.

"We need to talk."

Two minutes later, my new husband dismisses everyone at the party so that, finally, we are alone.

"What the actual fucking fuck was that shit show?"

Chapter Sixteen
River

"I have a wedding present for you, Tesoro." Marco grabs my hand—the not-slit-open-with-a-knife hand—and starts to lead me down the stairs, the smell of the night air immediately replaced by the unique scent that is Marco's home.

"Excuse me, Mr. Asshole, none of that blood shit was in our contract. Explain your-fucking-self, right now. I'm not going anywhere with you." Gripping the banister, I pull back from him, ripping my hand from his.

He stops and turns to face me, looking up at me on a higher step.

"It had to be done. Now come. Why are you always so resistant to my surprises?"

"Getting my hand sliced open is not the kind of surprise a girl dreams about for her wedding day." I sigh heavily, glaring at him in a way to make him understand I'm pissed about the whole hand slicing thing, which still stings like a bitch, even though it's now covered with a bandage matching Marco's. "Do you have any idea how fucking dangerous mixing blood is? How do I know you haven't infected me with some blood disease or some shit?

"Tesoro, you know I haven't. We've both been tested." Tugging at my hand, he tries to make me move from the spot I'm frozen on, and I'm dumbfounded that he thinks this was okay.

"I don't give a fuck that we've been tested, Marco. This isn't something I agreed to, and you damn well know it."

I'm immediately pushed against the banister, his arms either side of me, caging me in. "That mouth of yours is feral." A sly smile crosses his face as he leans in and bites my bottom lip, before pulling away and resting his forehead against mine. "As for what happened, it's in the contract. A contract you signed, and therefore agreed to."

"You know damn well that contract was doctored. I don't know how you did it, but half of the shit written in there, I would never agree to."

"I have no idea what you're talking about." Backing off of me, he grabs my hand again and begins to pull me down the stairs.

"This conversation isn't over."

"We'll see. Come on." Even his wink is fucking sexy. God damn this man.

As much as I'm pissed at Marco, and would love to knee him in the balls right now, I'm also curious as to what he has in store for our wedding night. Maybe it's his own special red room and he's about to get filthy as fuck. I'm aware this isn't where my mind should be going, but it's been a long-ass day, I'm tired, and I've already broken all my usual rules. It's like I'm an observer in my own mind, just here for the ride at this point.

"Ugh. You're incorrigible. Fine. But don't think I'm dropping the whole mutilation thing." Shoving past him, I roll my eyes and make my way down the stairs in front of him, the train of my dress flowing neatly behind me—which means the fucker has to walk a few steps behind me to avoid stepping on it.

"Five," is whispered into my ear as we reach the bottom before Marco takes my hand again and pulls me toward the door I know leads to the basement. It's just past his office door, the one place I've stayed away from since the meeting with Mr. Bobby's lawyer. Mainly because it's where Marco seems to conduct most of his business, and while he's in there, he's leaving me alone. Admittedly, I am still constantly supervised by Stefano, Enzo, or Lina. Sometimes

Luca, but he's not here very often and when he is, he spends most of his time in the kitchen preparing meals.

"Is my wedding present all the spanking you've been threatening? Because if it is, it's not much of a surprise, and I can't say I'm all that excited about it." I'm lying, of course. I'm actually a little wet just thinking about it.

Once we reach the door to the basement, he spins me so my back is against the frame, his hands on either side of my head, caging me in. Within seconds, his lips are on mine in a hungry kiss that doesn't last long enough before he pulls away.

"My wedding present may be a little... unconventional. But it is exactly what you need, Tesoro."

His steel-gray eyes are so intense as he meets my gaze, I'd go so far as to say they're a little scary.

"Marco, nothing about you is conventional. I'm sure I can handle whatever kinky surprise you've got for me."

A brief sadness crosses his face, but it's quickly replaced by the same intensity from before as he reaches down to open the door behind me. He walks me carefully through the door and down the stairs backward, his hands on the tops of my arms as he guides me down. I can hear a deep muffled laugh behind me, which makes me even more curious. Marco told me he doesn't share, so this isn't about to be the sex-fest I'd expected. There's a crinkling of some kind of material as we move into the room, which confuses me even more.

"Turn around." He's so serious, maybe he's worried I won't like what he's planned. Which actually makes me a little nervous.

Doing as he says, I look to the floor and slowly turn—wanting to get the full effect when I look up—and Marco's grip on me moves to my hips. Closing my eyes, I move my head up before opening them to see…

"Oh my God, Marco, what the fuck have you done? I know him. Let him go!" Pushing Marco's hands away from me, I run to the chair in the middle of the room, immediately spinning it so I can begin to untie him.

Then my nose is assaulted with the smell of nicotine, and the night in the alley comes rushing back to me. No…

I spin the chair again so I'm facing him, my breaths coming short and fast as tears sting my eyes. In this moment, staying strong in front of my client can go fuck itself. Everything around me blurs and I focus on the man in the chair.

"Tell me it wasn't you, Frank."

A gruesome smile appears through the gag on his battered and bloody face. My whole body is shaking with adrenaline and I have no fucking idea what's going on right now.

Heat warms my back as Marco moves to stand behind me, and I feel him place something cold into my right hand.

"I know what he did to you, Tesoro. Now it's time for you to take your power back from this vermin."

Looking down, I see a beautiful diamond-encrusted dagger in my hand, which I immediately drop in shock.

What the fuck does Marco expect me to do?

"You need this." His breath tickles my ear as he speaks in a low, deep grumble, then he spins me to face him once again.

I'm trembling with fear, anger, confusion... so many things, I can't pinpoint just one.

"Marco, what the actual fuck?"

"This man is responsible for your torment. He's been calling you, sending you messages, and he's responsible for your Mr. Bobby. Vincenzo has been on the hunt and we finally tracked him down."

"No..."

"Tesoro—"

"That's not all he's responsible for." The anger inside me is taking precedence over my other emotions. The night in the alley, clear as day in my mind's eye.

I'm not a violent person, I'd rather poke myself in the eye than hurt an insect on purpose, but this... this might just change me. Marco's right. As much as the asshat who stole a patch of my skin seems to be where all this started, the calls have been going on for much longer. Frank may be the one who un-dicked the asshat—if what he said in the alley was true—but he's also the one who scarred my face, has me walking faster at night, and now I find out he killed Mr. Bobby.

The afternoon in Polly's office replays in my mind, the way his face screwed up when I turned him down, the way his fists clenched at my refusal.

"What else is he responsible for? Use it, Tesoro."

"I... He..."

Argh, I want to scream at myself. The words catch in my throat, unmoving.

"Breathe with me. In... Out..."

Marco is surprisingly calm considering there's a bloody man tied to a chair in the middle of his basement. But then, after the whole ritual thing at the wedding, I'm pretty sure I have put myself into a fucked-up situation with fucked-up people.

This is why I research.

I follow Marco's lead, breathing in and out as he does, and it calms me a little. Then the sound of Frank's heavy breaths invades my ears and makes my skin crawl with a hatred I've never felt before. It's completely foreign to me, but as Marco grips my chin and forces me to look up at him, I calm.

"What did he do?"

With another deep breath, I try to find the words. Obviously, being attacked in an alley isn't quite on the same level as an attempted murder on me, only for my friend to be killed instead, but it was fucking traumatic, and I never want to feel that kind of weakness again.

"He... he did this"—I move a hand to my eyebrow—"on the night he ambushed me on my way home."

Marco's eyes turn to fire and his grip on my chin tightens, but not to the point of pain.

"Then I have been too kind to our friend here."

His hand moves up and I screech when I hear a gunshot, followed by Frank's muffled scream. Spinning around, I see a new bloodied hole in his shin. I look down and see a gun in Marco's hand, the sight driving me away from him, speechless.

"I will leave the rest to you, Tesoro. He is your gift. How he dies tonight is your choice."

Fucking die?

"Marco, this… it's too much. This isn't me. I can't. You have to let me leave."

"I will give you the world, but this is something you need to heal. So you will stay right here beside me, as my queen, and you will show yourself how strong I know you are."

"I don't know what you want from me." My body is on fire, my lungs struggling for breath again.

"Yes, you do."

Marco bends to pick up the dagger I dropped, and places it back in my hand. He curls my fingers around the handle and keeps his hand over mine as he turns me once again to face Frank.

This isn't right. It's all kinds of wrong and I need to find a way out.

"Enzo, remove the gag."

I didn't even realize he was in the room with us, but he appears from the shadows in the corner of the room and does as instructed, removing the black material from Frank's mouth. Frank splutters and spits, before that maniacal smile crosses his face once again, showing his blood-covered teeth.

"Now leave us." As silently as he appeared, Enzo leaves the room.

"You'll never be anything more than a fucking whore. You were supposed to love me, you ungrateful slut. That old man may have saved your shitty little life, but you'll have to live with knowing it's all your fault. If it wasn't for you, he would still be alive." Frank laughs, ending with a fluidy cough and a grin I want to wipe off his ugly face.

I can't believe I trusted this man, Polly trusted this man with all her girls. She's going to be devastated. How many others has he behaved like this with?

"Use his words, Tesoro."

Frank laughs once again. "How much is this one paying you, slut?"

Marco's hand is still over mine, holding the dagger with me as I tentatively step closer to the chair.

"That's it. Now, what do you want to do?" His voice in my ear sends a lustful shiver up my spine, but that's as fucked-up as this situation, so I tamp it down. This is not the time.

"This is all wrong. I..."

"Let me help."

We move forward as one, closer to the bleeding man in the chair, and Marco moves my hand up, the dagger now resting against Frank's throat.

"I don't know what I ever saw in you. You're weak, pathetic, ungratef—"

Something comes over me with Frank's words as they turn into more of a gargle, and it's not Marco, it's me who's pushing the dagger into his skin, causing blood to pool at the new opening.

"That's it, Tesoro."

My hand is shaking now, the reality of what's happening is starting to come back to me and I'm scared about how right this feels.

Marco steadies me and slowly guides my hand across Frank's throat, the dagger creating a bloody line as it moves. It's not as easy as it looks in the movies, there's a little more resistance as it goes over his Adam's apple.

I should look away, be sick, run, scream, cry... anything other than what I'm doing right now, which is staring at the bloody mess in front of me as the life leaves Frank's eyes. The universe is going to send me some shitty karma to make up for this. Then again, maybe I am the karma. Frank has been an evil, nasty man, and I never would have known if it wasn't for Marco.

I feel stronger and weaker all at the same time. My body sags back against Marco and my grip on the dagger loosens. It falls from my fingers as Marco catches me and I turn into his chest. One palm rests against my head while the other rubs up and down my back, and for the first time in too long, I allow my tears to fall.

After a few minutes, Marco places his hands on either side of my head and moves me to look up at him.

"Your tears are beautiful, Tesoro."

A need builds in my stomach as I stare into his deep gray eyes full of respect, then I glance at his mouth and find myself grabbing at his shirt, pulling him onto me. I attack his mouth with the same desperation he always seems to claim me with, pushing all my shitty emotions aside so I can feel something good, something I can control.

I search his tongue out with mine, nipping at it and sucking on his bottom lip as his hands move from my head, over my shoulders, down my back and rest on my ass. He squeezes, making me groan into his mouth, and my hands grip at his hair, holding him close to me.

Wrapping my legs around his waist as he lifts me, I feel his thick, hard cock against my ass, sending flutters through my clit.

"Fuck me." They're barely words, but I say them like my life depends on it in between rough kisses and nips.

"As you wish, Tesoro."

Marco walks with me in his arms, slamming my back into the door and moving my dress up my legs so he has better access. He holds me with one arm, and unbuttons his pants with the other, then moves my panties aside and slams right into me in one deep thrust. I'm wet enough to fill the Nile, so his cock slides in like it was always meant to be there.

"Yes!" I scream into his ear as I grip onto him, allowing him to fuck me with abandon.

He slams in and out of me, kissing and licking at my neck, and rubbing at my clit with his free hand, the other gripping at my thigh—which will no doubt bruise, but I don't give a shit.

"Don't come yet," he growls into my ear before biting my lobe, and I groan loudly at the order and sensations all rolling into one.

"Please, Marco."

"Not yet."

In, out, in, out, bite, lick, flick, pinch... it's all too much yet not enough.

"Oh God, Marco, please."

His grunts at my ear are causing my nipples to pebble against the material of my dress, rubbing against it and making my insides bubble and build with pleasure. He moves his hand from my clit to my throat, holding me in place as he attacks my mouth once more, biting my bottom lip before licking the pain away.

"Come for me now, Tesoro."

The pressure on my chest and throat from his hand is intoxicating. Mixed with the deep thrusts and his order for me to come, I don't think twice. I let the building orgasm free, feeling myself pulse against him as his movements become erratic and he joins me with one last push, his deep growl sending a thrill down my spine. My entire body tingles, sensitive to every touch on my skin, and Marco kisses me again, softer this time. Leaving me boneless in his arms.

As he pulls away, I notice the red on his shirt, where my hand had been, then I look at my own hand and see it's covered in blood, my dress completely ruined with the splatters of red. I almost gag at the sight until Marco grabs my hand and moves it down, pulling me in for another sensual kiss.

"You do not feel bad about any of this. It is not your fault."

I'm lost for words, confused about my own actions, confused about who Marco really is, and confused about the people I thought I could trust.

Today has been a lot. I'm married, Kai gave me away, my stalker has been found and I helped kill him. Then on top of all that, I had sex with my new husband while covered in another man's blood.

It's all a little bit too much, and I can feel my mind checking out, like this part of my life is some seedy motel where rooms are by the hour. I need to walk away, to put distance between me and this man I thought I understood. This client I thought I could trust. This madman who literally bloodied my hands. Most of all, I need to squash the small part of me that is grateful for him.

Marco's dick is still inside me, my legs still wrapped around his waist, as he opens the door and carries me upstairs.

I can't find the words to speak, so I stay silent and allow him to place me on his bed, remove my dress, and take me into the shower.

He sheds his own clothes before stepping inside with me, and slowly cleans away the blood and cum. It's not sexual, but as usual with Marco, it's everything I need.

Chapter
Seventeen
River

"I'm bored." Dressed like a boardroom executive, I'm at the threshold of Marco's office, leaning against his door jamb—arms crossed—determined to get my way. For once.

It turns out being a Regina—or queen of this fucking criminal world—is a lot of work, but today, no one is asking me to look at files and determine who needs help with what. Mostly, I take care of the Italian families that are struggling in the area.

With an entire team behind me, we find jobs or housing. We feed those who can't seem to make ends meet. When Marco told me about my role as the Regina, he gave me free rein over our kingdom. I have a budget and I have appointments with members of the community who come to us for help. The stories are sometimes heartbreaking, usually heartwarming. This job is like a calling for me, a way to absolve myself of this negative energy.

I get to bring good because, in this world, we take care of our own.

Unless you're killing them for revenge.

I ignore the voice in my head that's been wreaking havoc on my conscience, ignore the twisting in my lower belly every time the images of my wedding night assault me. To be fair, Marco has been my therapist in many ways, soothing my mind and battering my body with powerful orgasms. That night I screamed at him, slapped and punched him, insulted him over and over again and he let me. With his hands in his pockets, he allowed me to exhaust myself to the point of falling on the floor and sobbing. That's when he picked me up and sat me on his lap where he whispered in my ear. "There are no ends I won't go to, no lives I won't take, and no rules I won't shatter if it means you're safe. It's non-negotiable." I fell asleep in his arms and woke up the next morning with his cock buried in my pussy and his tongue coaxing my lips open.

"If you need more work, I'm sure I can find something for you to do." He pushes away from his desk, legs spread out and a grin so wicked it could make the devil jealous.

"I'm not sucking your dick."

"Maybe you should so my cum can cleanse that dirty mouth of yours." Goddamnit, how does he do this to me every time? His filthy mouth is a hot button to my aching clit.

"Maybe I'll just strip down to nothing and go see what Lucas is making for lunch." I begin to pop open my shirt but I don't get to the third button before Marco is right in my face, one hand grabbing the top of the door jamb, the other cupping my heated pussy.

"I don't think you want to play that game, Tesoro." Hmm, possessive Marco is the sexiest Marco of all. Although, playful Marco likes to spank me and workaholic Marco likes to fuck me in his big mafia boss chair.

"Then I suggest you entertain me. Who knows what your bored wife is capable of doing?" Without a moment's hesitation and with the dexterity of a man on a mission, Marco unfastens my pants—his hand diving in—and buries two fingers inside my aching pussy.

"My cunt. My orgasms. *E tutta mia.*" *It's all mine.* I've learned that phrase since he says it all the time.

"Yes!" It doesn't take long for my orgasm to build. In the month since our wedding, Marco has learned every inch of my body, every one of my erogenous zones, every plea that falls from my lips. My husband may be many things, but he's not a slacker when it comes to my pleasure.

"Who is allowed to see your tits, River?"

"You."

"*Bene*." Pushing the material aside, he sucks on the flesh of my breast before biting down on my nipple and soothing it with a wet, hot, lick.

"Who is allowed to see your cunt?"

"You." My hips are pushing at him, silently begging for more.

"*Bene*." Falling to his knees, he pulls my pants and underwear down as he goes and gives me exactly what I need, his mouth latching onto my clit and his fingers fucking me with precision.

It takes two minutes for my body to give in.

Piercing this all-consuming haze of lust with his gray eyes, Marco silently gives me permission to let go. And I do. I come all over his face and fingers and only when I fall to my own knees in front of him does he speak.

"Open." Without even questioning him, I open my mouth, allowing him to coat my lips with my cum before he leans in and kisses the arousal right off, leaving me breathless and a little bit in awe of his talents.

"Let's go out. I can't have my wife bored at home."

"Okay, I'll get cleaned up." His hand is quicker than lightning as his fingers grab my jaw and his wicked grin is the only thing in my line of sight.

"No. You're perfect just like this. I want every man that passes by to know you're wearing the orgasm I just gave you."

"A hotel? Really? You need to work on your wooing skills, Marco. No wonder you're paying me so much." Looking up at the intricacy of one of the most iconic buildings in New York City, a sudden wave of pride washes over me. Above the entrance in gold lettering and bold lines is the name Mancini. Proud and all-encompassing—standing tall among the mere mortals of Manhattan—is the luxury hotel where the rich and famous from all around the world pay exorbitant amounts of money to have the privilege of saying they stayed the night.

"That mouth, *Dolcezza*, is going to get you into a lot of trouble." Taking my hand, he rubs his thumb over my wedding band as he pulls me inside the golden double doors.

I grin at the doorman as Marco shakes his hand, asking him how his family is doing.

"Good, thank you, sir." I don't think my husband realizes how good he just made that man feel. It's like I can see his aura changing colors as we speak.

"Have you met my wife?" Pulling me closer, he introduces me to Emmett, who immediately bows his head in reverence. That act alone makes me extremely uncomfortable. I'm not a queen, no matter how many times the name Regina is thrown at me. I'm just a girl from Staten Island who was able to make ends meet by selling my only assets at the time.

Myself.

"It's a pleasure, Mrs. Mancini."

"The pleasure is mine, Emmett."

Marco shakes his hand again, a flash of green peeking out from the corner of his palm.

"Thank you, sir. Thank you. Have a great day."

Stepping inside, I'm overwhelmed by the elegance and beauty of the great hall. Everest would use the word opulence; the gold trimmings and expensive paintings lining the walls are probably worth more than all of our assets combined.

"This," Marco leads me to a shelf that looks like something out of a pre-war movie with round edges and burdensome history. Without touching it, he points to a clock encased in a glass cube, the face at the center with a golden harp on top and two cherubs standing on either side. It's gaudy and, frankly, ugly. But who am I to judge? "It belonged to my great-grandfather. Brought it over from Italy—Firenze—and when he first built this hotel, it was just a mom-and-pop little place with a few rooms." The pride in his voice is fascinating. I don't know much about my grandparents. My father had broken all ties in college when their political views clashed and he could no longer live under their strict rule.

I wish I had this much passion for my ancestry. At least I feel it for my immediate family, so there's that.

"So, you decided to keep it in the main hall as a reminder of your past?" Marco turns to me, his grin beautiful and infectious.

"The past dictates our fate and if there's one thing I've learned, it's that fate always wins."

"Whatever. I mean, I get it, but from an esthetic point of view, it breaks the lines of the great hall. Instead of bringing your clients' eyes to the vast beauty, it automatically falls on this." I shrug, not really knowing what the fuck I'm talking about. I barely have a high school diploma, let alone a degree in interior design.

"Maybe. Come, I want to show you something."

We head straight for the elevators where Marco takes out a special key and turns it on the lone double doors in the far back. The doors open immediately and once inside, it's clear this is a private shaft. With another turn of the key, the elevator takes off and only stops once.

"You do love your rooftops, don't you?" For the first time, I see Marco without his mask. I see the young man who has a passion, who has mischief written all over his bright, mesmerizing eyes.

"I really fucking do."

"Do I get to spank you for your filthy mouth, too?" With one hard yank, he has me flush against his body, his vanilla scent making my skin buzz with heat.

"I'd like to see you try." Raising a brow, I push up on my tiptoes and trap his bottom lip between my teeth, earning me a growl.

"Challenge accepted, Mr. Mancini."

With a turn of his heel, I'm suddenly facing away with my back to his front and my eyes landing on the most sought after view in the world.

"Holy shit, Marco."

"Yeah. A little piece of heaven for my queen."

Up here, some forty stories high in the dead of winter, I can see the whole of Manhattan. It's a three-sixty view with the highest skyscrapers towering over us like omens, but the park... it's straight out of a fairytale.

It's one thing when you see Central Park from behind the safety of a closed window, but an entirely different experience when you can practically smell the romance on every bridge and taste the sweat of every runner.

"I've never seen anything so beautiful." My eyes are trained on the view, the late-January sky heavy with the weight of the clouds, the wind chill multiplied by a hundred this far up.

"*Neanche io.*"

When I look back at Marco, he doesn't even pretend to be admiring the view. His eyes are on me, the gray skies a perfect match to his irises.

"What does that mean?"

"Me neither."

Wrapping his arms tighter around me, he leans closer to my ear and whispers, "The best part is about to start."

Placing both of his hands on my eyes, he chuckles as I curse his wicked ways. I'm about to pull his hands down to see what's going on but instead I just place them on top of his, the warmth of his skin so delightful.

"Ready?"

"Yes!"

His hands part, my eyes slowly opening and readjusting to the light.

A gasp is the only sound I hear when my eyes take in the sight before me. We're facing West, the sun falling just over the tallest skyscrapers sending beams of light across the park and into the mirrored windows of neighboring buildings. The reflections dance across the whole of Manhattan like a game of dominos. The oranges and reds and blues reflect off every surface of the island and as I stand there, it's like the sun is suffusing its energy right into me. Giving me strength and warmth. Filing me with an urgent sense of belonging.

"The sun is bowing at your feet, as it should. Always."

Chapter
Eighteen
River

Dressed in a stunning floor-length black gown with a high neck, my shoulders and back bare, and delicate crystals scattered from the waist down, I feel like the queen I'm pretending to be. Saying that though, I don't have my full Rose costume on because Marco refuses to allow me to wear a wig, so I'm missing a little of my usual armor, but I'm a professional so I can deal with it. We're at the most boring gala I think I've ever attended—and there have been a few, as this is where clients want the façade of success with a young woman hanging off of their every word.

The room itself is beautiful. Purple hues from the lighting reflect off every detailed surface inside the Angel Orensanz Foundation, and the balconies just below the high, domed ceilings are all decorated with bouquets of white and black flowers. Round tables are placed throughout the room, with white tablecloths and dressed chairs, almost like a wedding reception... only, this is a fundraiser for Senator Beckett's campaign. Someone who I know uses Polly's girls on a regular basis, as I remember seeing his name in her appointment book.

All of New York's elite are in attendance, it's an opportunity for the rich and seedy to rub shoulders and boast about all the money they're able to donate to worthless events like this. If it was a fundraiser for an actual charity, one that does some real good, I'd be all for it. But this is mainly a who's who of corrupt rich people.

Including my husband, who is apparently as corrupt as they come. The last two months with Marco have been a real eye-opener. The Mancinis may own a large chain of luxury hotels and help Italian families in need, but they're also into some shady shit. I mean, tying Frank up in a chair and having me slice his throat was a huge red flag the size of his ego.

As much as I know I should've walked away then and there, I didn't want to. Something inside of me wanted to stay, to see the situation through to the end, and once I did, a tiny piece of myself came back to me. It's fucked up as shit, but Marco's been like some kind of weird-ass therapy.

He forces me not to just face my fears, but to slaughter them—literally, it seems.

From a young girl playing in fields of flowers, surrounded by peace and love, I almost don't recognize myself anymore. The strange thing is, it doesn't feel as wrong as I know it should. I've allowed myself to become completely consumed by Marco and this lifestyle, but maybe that's because I know there's a time-limit.

Would I be behaving differently if this was a real forever? Probably.

Marco is talking to a man named Chase Kensington, who briefly introduced himself before dismissing me in favor of Marco's attention. Chase is some big money man in The City, and I'm surprised I've never worked for him or seen his name on Polly's books.

My eyes widen as I see someone I recognize heading this way and my grip on Marco's arm tightens.

"What's wrong, Tesoro?" Immediately, Marco pauses his conversation with Chase in favor of giving me his sole attention.

"Nothing." I smile sweetly up at him, because being a bitch in public isn't the image I agreed to give when signing the contract.

"Don't lie to me." He's being stern, but not angry, and I appreciate his self-restraint in public also.

"Dad, we need to talk." The guy I recognize addresses Chase before looking at Marco and me to apologize for interrupting. *I want to crawl into a hole.* Halfway through his apology, he pauses and glances in my direction before returning his attention to his dad.

A blonde guy I also recognize appears at his side moments later, and squints his eyes at me, tilting his head to the side as he asks, "Do I know you from somewhere?" Another appears moments later. The guy who looks like a bronzed god studies me intently before turning their inquisitive stare to Marco.

Marco's arm moves around my waist, and he pulls me closer to him, squeezing my hip.

"Not now, Travis. Find me later." Chase raises his voice before pulling himself back together, nodding his head politely at Marco as he turns to walk away.

"Hey, aren't you the girl with the phone?" The girl from the alley appears from behind the ripped, tall guy who interrupted us. I almost didn't recognize her. She looks so different. Her long dark hair is pinned away from her face and falls in waves down her back. Her midnight-blue gown is so dark it almost looks black, despite the shimmer that makes the dress look like she's wrapped in the night sky. She's a long way from the casual girl who saved me.

I relax under Marco's hold, remembering now that these are the guys who helped me the night in the alley, and not some crazy ex-client—which is a huge possibility in my line of work.

"I am. Thank you for all your help. My name's River by the way, much better than *girl with the phone* I think." A real smile forms on my lips for the first time so far this evening. I like this girl's energy. "You're Briar, right?" I know I had other things on my mind that night, but I'm in a better place now—albeit it a fucked up one—and I want to thank this girl and her men properly.

Marco stands stoically by my side, like he's now my arm candy instead of the other way around.

"I am. This is Travis," she says motioning to Chase's son. "Sawyer St. Vincent and Cole Beckett. And who is this?"

She eyes Marco up and down, in a completely non-sexual way, but we're girls, we speak the same code. I know she thinks he's hot, same as the men she introduced to me, but we don't say that out loud. Honestly, you'd think we were in a lion's den with the feral noises the guys are making.

"The growly man with a tight grip on my waist is Marco." She smirks at me, like she understands the growly thing a little too well as Travis pulls her into his side.

"Marco Mancini. Her husband." I almost falter at the word husband. Almost.

The guy she called Travis raises his eyebrows in what looks like recognition or respect at Marco's name before stepping forward to shake his hand.

"Travis Kensington."

"These are the guys I told you about, they found my keys and phone." I don't want to get into specifics right now, because that would be awkward as fuck, so I'm hoping what I'm saying jogs Marco's memory of the night I told him what happened in the alley.

"Chase's son?" Marco's eyes narrow in on Travis, questioning.

"Not that I like to admit it, but yeah."

"Can't say you got dealt the honorable dad card."

Travis smiles. "You can say that again."

He turns to the twins, a small smile on his face. "I know your mother too, I believe. St. Vincent you said?" The more playful one nods as Marco turns to Cole. "And I assume you're the senator's son?"

The giant beefcake nods once, not even a hint of a smile on his chiseled face and Marco relaxes beside me, his tense posture easing slightly. "Thank you for what you did for my wife. If you ever need a favor, here's my card."

Okay, so a favor from Mr. Mancini is a lot more thanks than I had planned to give, but there it is.

Another guy—I'm assuming the twin of the blonde because it's that or I'm seeing double—comes up behind Briar and slides his hand around to her stomach, whispering in her ear. When I thought they were all her guys, I didn't realize they were her… *guys*. I had thought they were all just really good friends, but damn, lucky girl.

"Thank you, Mr. Mancini. We may take you up on that offer sooner rather than later." Briar answers, taking the card while Travis grips her waist tighter. I might have missed it if I wasn't so used to paying attention to body language. He obviously knows Marco, but maybe he knows too much. He leans down and whispers in her ear, and she rolls her eyes so hard I worry a little for her.

"Sorry River, we've got to go. Give me a call whenever though. Sometimes we girls just need a chat that doesn't involve all the peen."

They turn and leave as quickly as they arrived, filtering through the crowd. Briar is quite a few years younger than me, but she comes across as an older soul. I like her, she's ballsy.

"You didn't need to do that. I can handle my own shit."

Marco pulls me into him, my back to his front as he strokes his hand down the side of my face, across my shoulder and over my arm, reaching my hand and interlinking his fingers with mine.

"I know. But you're mine, and we come as a package deal now."

"Only for another month." I say the words, barely above a whisper, but he hears them and spins me to face him. His eyes look dangerous, and his lips are tilted up only ever so slightly at the corners as he lifts my hand to his mouth, placing a soft kiss on my wedding band.

"We'll see."

Before I have a chance to respond, he begins to lead me toward the bar in the corner of the room. There are too many people around for me to argue with him like I want to, and the fucker knows it.

"Lina?" She's leaning against the bar, and the silhouette of a man I know very well is talking to her with his back to us. "What are you doing here? You're supposed to be in Monaco."

Her face pales, briefly, before a blush begins to creep up her chest, almost matching the scarlet of the beautiful gown she's wearing. "Hey, Marco. I came back early. Surprise!"

The guy moves to stand beside Lina, resting his elbows on the tall bar behind him.

"Tyler."

"Marco."

They shake hands and do the whole *pat each other on the back* thing that men do sometimes.

"You were in Monaco this week, weren't you?"

The impenetrable mask that is Tyler fucking Walker, falters briefly before he reins it in. Not a lot can pierce his facade, but it seems Marco Mancini is one of those things that can.

"I was."

I'm not sure whether a fight is about to break out or not, because from what I'm hearing, Tyler and Lina were in Monaco together. I don't feel the pang of jealousy I felt when I heard about Kai's engagement. Instead, I'm just happy for them both. Lina is a beautiful soul, and Tyler could really use a strong woman like her in his life. The way he looks at her reminds me of Ev and Petal. I'm ready to defend their budding love if Marco decides to go all batshit on us, but he surprises me yet again.

"You look after her with your life, protect her, worship the ground she fucking walks on. Because she deserves nothing less. I don't need to tell you what would happen if you hurt her, so we'll leave it at that... Brother."

"Understood."

Men are such strange creatures. All their posturing and threats, it's like something from an animal documentary.

I make eye contact with Lina, raising a brow at her in surprise and mouthing, "wow." She doesn't need to hear from me that I used to sleep with her new boyfriend, and though I'm sure Marco knows I did, he's also choosing to ignore that in favor of their pending love. Which is pretty sweet, considering he's usually a giant asshole.

"I need the bathroom. River, you coming?" I'm not usually a 'girls go to the bathroom in packs' kinda girl, but for Lina, and this juicy gossip she no doubt has, I'll make an exception.

"Sure."

Marco pulls me into him for a long, slow, devouring kiss, accompanied by words of discouragement from his sister, before letting me go. He pats me on the ass as I walk away, and I've got to say, I've begun to quite like it.

After hearing all about Tyler and Lina's budding relationship, which is a whole story in itself, I realize I really need to use the toilet. Lina is eager to get back to Tyler, so I tell her to go while I sort myself out.

As I exit the bathroom, someone grabs my arm and pulls me to the side, pushing me against the wall. It's not rough or hard, but the flashbacks to the night in the alley are real. My breathing speeds up and I lose focus on my surroundings for a moment.

"River. Listen to my voice..." He places my hand on his chest and takes deep breaths, encouraging me to follow. "That's it, Skittles. There you are."

"Nathaniel?" I'm either hallucinating, or Nathaniel is really in front of me, one hand on my head, the other holding mine to his chest. "What are you doing here?" This gala is becoming an awkward-as-fuck walk down memory lane.

"My mother is a benefactor to the Senator. She needed a date." His blue eyes focus on my green ones, and I wish I could take back what happened, apologize... something. But I can't say anything because of my contract with Marco. Which is frustrating as fuck.

Mr. Bobby's voice echoes in my mind. *Big picture.*

"That was nice of you. And I'm good now, thank you. You can let me go."

Something passes over his eyes that I can't describe, but it's gone before I can analyze it properly.

"Why haven't you called me, Skittles?"

"Look, Nathaniel, I wish I could tell you I'm sorry, but I can't right now. One day, I can explain everything, but n—"

"You're making a big mistake." His interruption is welcome, because I don't know where I was going with my weak explanation of nothingness.

"Probably."

Tugging my hand free of his, and with one, last longing look into his beautiful baby blues, I walk away... and smack into a hard, toned chest. Marco.

"Are you okay, Tesoro? You were gone for a while."

His features morph instantly from worried to angry as his gaze travels over my shoulder to the man standing behind me. He's definitely jumping to conclusions if a talk with an ex is making him that mad. Although, I also can't blame him, it wasn't exactly a normal and friendly talk.

Marco breathes heavily out of his nose as Nathaniel passes us with a smug look I haven't seen on him before.

Seething with anger, he digs his fingers at my waist as he tries to contain his sudden rage. And ever the professional, I stroke my fingers through his hair the way he likes, to soothe him. At least that's what I'm telling myself, it's for him, not me. It's part of the contract.

"Fucking Nathaniel."

Chapter
Nineteen
River

Last night was a cluster fuck of epic proportions.

In public, we were the perfect couple. Touching and whispering in each other's ears with loving smiles plastered on our faces. Except, if anyone took a microscope to us, they would have known that our whispers were of me telling Marco to stop being a jealous asshole. And Marco grunting his frustration. They would have seen that his smile was actually a scowl and his loving touches were nothing more than possessive posturing.

As soon as the door to our car closed behind us, the façade was dropped and the silence came hard and fast. Needless to say, I slept in my own bedroom instead of sharing a bed with his broody majesty.

Today, though, I feel a little guilty. I mean, he knows there's a past with Nathaniel and if I can explain things there may very well be a future with him. But none of this makes sense. I get it, anyone could have walked in on me talking to Nathaniel, which would have put our sham of a marriage at the mercy of high-society scrutiny.

Still, instead of sulking, he could talk like an adult.

After showering and dressing in the most comfortable clothes I own, I make my way to the kitchen for some much needed coffee and breakfast. It may be mid-February outside but in our home, the temperature is perfect. No slippers needed with a plush carpet such as this one.

"What the fuck, Marco? You're going off script." Enzo sounds worried, pissed off, even.

"Don't worry about me, just make sure I have all the fucking information I need." I should probably make my entrance instead of eavesdropping on what is surely a conversation about business. Whatever the fuck that may be.

"I'm telling you, this is a bad idea."

"Get me the details. I want to know everything. Where he is, what he's doing, when he eats and when he fucking shits. I want all of it." I've never heard Marco this worked up. He prides himself on his control but clearly, he's losing it right now.

"Is everything okay?" I walk in like a fresh flower and not at all like someone who's been listening to a private conversation.

Enzo looks over at me, almost apologetically, while Marco barely acknowledges my presence.

Asshole.

"Okay. So, I'm just going to grab a cup of coffee and you boys can resume..." I wave my hands in the air to describe whatever the fuck was going on since words escape me. "This whole thing."

I'm not used to this. In our family, silence isn't something we do. We talk, we work out our problems. We solve our disagreements. This separation of church and state—church being our relationship and state his business—is the most frustrating part of playing the role of Marco Mancini's wife.

Just as I'm about to walk out, I hear Enzo's not so whispered words.

"You have to fucking tell her."

I freeze. Marco curses under his breath and I'm guessing Enzo is going to get his ass kicked for that stunt.

"Tell me what?"

"Go back to your room, *Dolcezza*." He sips his coffee like everything is just fine and all I need to do is follow his orders. Yeah, I don't think so.

"Tell me what, Marco?" I'm closer to him now. Practically in his face as Enzo leaves the kitchen after dropping a bomb.

"You don't need to concern yourself with my business." Face to face, our jaws clenched and our eyes narrowed, it's clear neither one of us is going to back down. This just escalated from the silent treatment to a full-blown argument.

"Enzo said I need to know something so just fucking tell me."

"Watch your mouth."

"Fuck you. You watch *your* fucking mouth. If this has to do with me, then you need to act like a fucking adult and communicate." In two seconds flat, I'm turned around with my chest and face slamming into the kitchen counter and my legs spread wide enough to accommodate his size.

I feel his breath before I hear his words at my ear.

"When I tell you to watch your mouth. You watch your fucking mouth." Grabbing at the waist of my yoga pants, he pulls them down along with my underwear and traps my ankles with them.

"Fuck you."

"When I tell you to walk away, you walk. The fuck. Away." The sound of his belt sliding from the loops of his jeans has me both panting with need and gasping in shock.

He wouldn't.

With one hand keeping me down on the counter, he gives himself enough room to...

Slap.

I'm too stunned to respond, the stinging burn on my ass cheek silencing me immediately.

"How many fucking times have I told you to watch your filthy mouth?"

Slap. Slap.

My hands are grasping at nothingness as I try to hold myself still while my fucking husband literally spanks my ass.

I want to be disgusted—and on some level I think I may be—but the truth of the matter is that every time his leather belt connects with my skin, I feel my body leaning closer to him. Almost begging for more. My only hope is that he doesn't reach out and touch my pussy.

"Fucking Christ, look at you. You're wet for me. Your cunt is begging for my cock, isn't it?"

I shake my head, denying his accusation, but my body is betraying my mind and actions.

"Don't fucking lie to me, River. I don't do well with lies and omissions."

Slap. Slap.

Fuck, it hurts. And feels so fucking good.

"Were you counting down the days before you could return to Nathaniel Reed? Were you two planning our divorce so you could run back to him?"

Slap. Slap.

He's making no sense, but my mind *is* a bit muddled at this point.

"If you only fucking knew—" he cuts himself off as he buries two fingers inside my pussy. We both groan at the feel, my body aching for more.

"Knew what, Marco?"

Without giving me an answer, he expertly replaces his fingers with his rock-hard cock, deep and all-consuming, all the way to the hilt.

Panting, he covers my back with his front as he stays buried inside me.

"I don't share, Tesoro. Not anything and especially not you."

I could lie to myself and say he's talking on a professional level, but it feels different. It feels personal.

It feels real, somehow.

"Marco."

As though he regrets showing me this vulnerable side of him, he pulls out and slams right back inside me. Fucking me like a punishment and holding me like a lifeboat.

He's both hurting me and pleasuring me.

He's the yin to his own yang, a contradiction with every one of his movements.

I'm so close to losing my own control, close to coming all over his pistoning cock, that I almost miss his change in rhythm.

My ears are ringing with the force of his fucks but I'm sure the sound I'm hearing is him rummaging through the drawers at his side and the cupboards above us. What the fuck?

From the corner of my eye, I see him reach for a green bottle and realize it's olive oil.

"Marco?"

Without answering me, he uses one hand to unscrew the bottle and suddenly the thick liquid is pouring down the crack of my ass.

"Marco, what are you doing?" My voice is urgent, my ass cheeks stinging from the force of his belt, my pussy clenching around his thick cock, begging him to move, to thrust, to fuck me harder and faster.

"You're so beautiful like this, Tesoro. Naked and at my mercy. Scared and aroused all at the same time." More oil is poured over my ass cheeks and back to my asshole again before he returns the bottle to the counter.

One finger slides into my puckered hole with little resistance, his fondness for butt plugs making a whole lot of sense right now.

Two fingers in and he still hasn't moved his cock. Where the fuck does he get the restraint to sit fully inside me while playing with my hole?

My walls are squeezing his dick, all those Pilates classes coming in quite handy right about now.

"Fuck, do that again. Squeeze my dick, River. Beg. Me. For my cock." It's like he's unhinged yet completely in control of his actions. Like every time he's clenched his fists and his jaw it was a warning for this very moment.

Three fingers and the tightness from the invasion is so uncomfortable I'm afraid his cock will slide right out.

Pushing his fingers all the way inside, he reaches back for the bottle and pours a steady stream of olive oil all over my ass again. We're slippery, our clothes ruined, my mind on overdrive as he leans in and growls.

"Your cunt is mine." Pulling out, he slams back in so hard my entire body slides over the counter, my head tapping the wall. "This ass is mine."

That's when my doubts become truths.

Every nerve ending in my body lights up like a fucking Fourth of July fireworks festival. My skin is buzzing, my heart rate threatening to burst through my rib cage, my knees weak from the awkward position. Yet... I want it. I want to feel him own me in the one place I've let no one possess me.

But I can't.

Can I?

What does that mean if I give in to him? What does it say about this whole situation?

"Say it, River. Say the fucking words."

"No." God yes, please.

"Tell me this cunt is mine." One hand reaches up to my shoulder to hold me down, his grip hindered by the amount of oil on my skin.

"It's yours, Marco. My cunt is yours." I can barely breathe, the need to get fucked and to come is an all-time high.

"Tell me this ass is mine." He thrusts his fingers back in at the same time as his balls slap against my skin. He's fully enveloped by me, my body aching for more.

But if I tell him, I'm giving him permission to take everything I have.

Every fucking thing.

But fuck, I need to come so badly, I can taste it on my tongue.

No. I can't give him this. It's not his to own.

But my mouth betrays me.

"My ass is yours."

Everything happens so quickly. Pulling out of my pussy, he aligns himself with my ass, and just as he pulls out his fingers, the head of his cock slowly pushes in. Achingly slow.

Like he's teasing me. Punishing me more than he already has.

"Goddammit, Marco. Just fuck me already." The pressure is one thing, the burn from the belt is just added sensation to an already-erotic scene. But the sting from the sheer size of his cock trying to push through a small hole is almost agony.

Sweet, unadulterated agony.

Pulling me down by the shoulder, he warns me before he tears me apart.

"Brace yourself, Tesoro. Remember this as the precise moment you became mine in every fucking way."

Without stopping, he presses his body closer and closer to mine as his dick slides deeper and deeper into my ass until all I can feel is the fullness of him and the bite of pain from his entrance. My breaths are coming in heavy and fast, my pussy feels empty, bereft of his possession. But my ass? It wants more. It fucking needs more.

"Give it to me."

I have no idea who this woman crying out to him is. Who this person demanding to be fucked in the ass truly is. But I refuse to fight her.

I fucking need this.

"My pleasure," is all he says as he gives me exactly what I begged for all along. Wrapping his hand around my throat, he pulls me up to a straighter position as his dick pummels in and out of my ass, his filthy words like fuel to my raging fire.

"You like that, you dirty girl? You like feeling my cock owning you? Did you think you could ever leave me?"

In and out, screams pour out of my mouth every time he hits that sweet spot I didn't even know existed.

"Did you think I'd ever let you go?"

Oh, God. I need to come.

As though he can read my mind, he takes my hand—the one with the wedding band—and places it on my clit, rubbing it with me like I'm the puppet and he's my master.

"You ready, Tesoro?"

"God, yes!"

Releasing my hand, he buries more fingers than I dare to count inside my cunt and fucks both of my holes until I can't see. I can't speak. My mouth drops open in a silent cry of ecstasy, my knees no longer able to hold me up.

I come so hard, I think I actually lose consciousness.

Marco pulls out and just when I think he's done, he surprises me again by coming all over my skin. The burn that had subsided returns with a vengeance, reminding me that this all started because he deems my mouth filthy.

When truly, the filthy mouth is all his.

Turning to face him, I want to speak but my mouth won't open. My words refuse to be voiced.

Marco stares down at me, his face an impassive wall of emotions I don't understand. We're both silent as the enormity of this moment settles on us.

Reaching for the bottom drawer, he pulls out a dish towel.

"Marco!" Enzo's voice echoes in the next room and I stiffen with shame.

"Clean yourself up." Those are the last words I hear as he walks out of the kitchen without even a word over his shoulder.

I'm in shock. What the fuck is happening? Why is he like this?

Before he has time to go too far, I pull up my yoga pants and run out of the kitchen, screaming at him.

"Why are you acting like this? What is wrong with you?"

Marco freezes, his back to me, as Enzo turns and looks at me with a heartfelt apology. When Marco turns to face me, I feel cracks open where I thought my heart was locked tight.

"This is who I am, River. We have a contract, you signed willingly. Now do your fucking job."

With my mouth hanging open, my jaw slack from the shock of his words—his attitude, the cold tone of his voice—I stand there long enough to know he's left the building completely.

In the last two months, I've been the sole focus of this man's attention. Not only has he treated me like his queen, he's made sure everyone around us treated me as such. Yet, in this moment, I've never felt more like a whore.

Until now, I made my own decisions, played by my own rules. Rules I put in place to avoid this, avoid these painful feelings.

Rules he's broken over and over again since the day I met him.

This isn't who I am. Definitely not the person I aspire to be. As unconventional and scandalous as my job may be, I've always taken pride in how I choose my clients. How I help those who come to me.

Until this day, this very moment, I've always had respect for myself. Respect for my decisions.

Yet here I am, a couple of months into this job and I don't recognize myself. I have no idea who this person I've become truly is.

How did I end up so broken in such a short amount of time?

Lost in my own self-pity, I walk back to my room, take out my only bag and pack a few of my clothes. Adding my toiletries, I look around the bathroom to make sure I haven't forgotten anything. The nightstand is bare except for a book on the Mancini family sitting proudly on top.

My hand reaches for my left ring finger, carefully pulling the beautiful jewelry off and placing both the engagement ring and the wedding band on top of the book, right next to the name they truly belong to.

Tomorrow, I'll send the money right back to the sender, but for now I'm going to the only place I feel loved.

I'm going home.

To be continued in The Broken One
https://geni.us/TheBrokenOne

The Blonde One

Third time lucky? Nope. We're still keeping you guessing as to who River's Forever One will be. Will you be cursing our anonymous names? Probably... :)
Will you want to continue reading the final three books? We certainly hope so!
The Filthy One took us on a wild ride. Brunette had a thought, and we expanded on that, did some planning... then the planning threw itself out of the window and some shit happened. We both went totally off script and allowed the characters to lead us, and we really love what transpired. Even though we both cried super hard at the one chapter we shall not speak of...
You may recognize some characters in this book from a fabulous RH author—of which we are not—and she had her input on them, so they are a true likeness to how she has written them.

Once again, thank you to our families for understanding we each have a new family member now. Our fabulous editor, David... I'm so sorry! Brunette said, "He won't like it." I said, "Let's do it anyway." But we love you very much and you are all kinds of awesome, even though you may no longer be our fellow DJ.

And from Blondie to Brunette, I'm always going to be thankful that you said yes :)

THE BRUNETTE ONE

What can I say? This book was planned and plotted just like the other two but one thing is clear, the original plot went out the window the moment Marco Mancini came into the picture. He is no one's puppet, not even his creators'. I mean, I'm not complaining because I love him so much but he was difficult to control which as an author is quite amazing.

The chapter that shall not be named was difficult to write because we loved him so much but the sacrifice was needed for the Big Picture.

I know we're keeping you guessing but if it's any reassurance, we can say this... you've met River's forever one, the question is... which one?

When Blondie and I began this adventure, we didn't know how the readers would react to a serial, a series of books where we kept you guessing. Our main focus is River and her journey through life and death. We wanted to bring you a female lead that inspires and empowers our readers. She's not perfect but her heart is pure no matter how much her men try to dirty it up.

And no matter what, we truly believe her Forever one is perfect for her.

So, thank you for continuing the adventure with us, it's everything we hoped and dreamed it could be. Your support is everything to us.

To Blondie... from Brunette—saying yes was the easiest decision I've ever made. Fancy sticking around with me?

BOOKS BY N.O. ONE

Dark Contemporary Romance

The Escort Series (MF)

The Rich One ~ https://geni.us/TheRichOne

The Kinky One ~ https://geni.us/TheKinkyOne

The Filthy One ~ https://geni.us/TheFithyOne

The Broken One ~ https://geni.us/TheBrokenOne

The Almost One ~ https://geni.us/TheAlmostOne

The Forever One ~ https://geni.us/TheForeverOne

The Christmas One ~ Prequel to The Escort Series

KOK (RH)

Kings of Kink ~ https://geni.us/KingsOfKink

The Reapers Mafia Crew Duet (MF)

One Kill ~ https://geni.us/TheReapers1

One Love ~ https://geni.us/TheReapers2

The Psycho Trilogy – Sons of Khaos (MF)

Psycho Hate ~ https://geni.us/PsychoHate

Psycho Love ~ https://geni.us/PsychoLove

Psycho Reign ~ https://geni.us/PsychoReign

A Night To Remember Auction (MF)

Fatal

Sons of Khaos – The Standalones

Bear Hunt (MF) ~ https://geni.us/SOKBearHunt

Meat Grinder (Poly with MF and MM)

7 Deadly Sins – A Shared World

Gluttony (Why choose)

Next Door

The Assassin Next Door (MF)

Dark Paranormal Fantasy Romance

Society Of Soulkeepers

Hack (MF) ~ Book 1 of The White Horse Duet

Hex (MF) ~ Book 2 of The White Horse Duet

If you'd love to get in touch or find out more about our

books, please feel free to stalk us in all the places and join

our newsletter.

www.author-no-one.com

If you'd love to get in touch or find out more about our books, please feel free to stalk us in all the places and join our newsletter.

Here is our linktree: https://linktr.ee/n.o.one

BOOKS WE THINK YOU SHOULD READ

Dark Romance

DATE WITH THE DEVIL (MF) ~
HTTPS://GENI.US/DWTD

Contemporary

THE UCC SAGA
DISHEVELED ~ HTTP://AMZN.TO/2ARPBXP
DISARMED ~ HTTP://AMZN.TO/2MYVXNN
DISCARDED ~ HTTPS://AMZN.TO/2VWTRPF
UCC BOXSET ~ HTTPS://AMZN.TO/3LJVEPE

STANDALONE
THE WISH ~ HTTPS://AMZN.TO/2FTIKQB

Rom-Com

THE WOOLF FAMILY SERIES
SCREWED ~ HTTPS://GENI.US/SCREWED
SCREWED UP ~ HTTPS://BIT.LY/3IBFWKB
SCREWED OVER (COMING SOON)

Supernatural

SOUL GUARDIANS SERIES
REPRISE ~ HTTPS://BIT.LY/3CT9NPE

Eva LeNoir
Fun Flirty Romance

BY LILY WILDHART

Dark Romance

The Saints of Serenity Falls series (RH)
(You will find crossovers from The Escort series by N.O.
One in the Serenity Falls series by Lily Wildhart, and vice
versa!)
A Burn So Deep ~ https://geni.us/burnaltcover
A Revenge So Sweet ~ https://geni.us/revengealtcover
A Taste Of Forever ~ https://geni.us/tastealtcover

Website & Newsletter: www.author-no-one.com

Facebook: https://geni.us/Facebookauthor

Facebook Group: https://geni.us/FierceReaders

Instagram: https://geni.us/Instagramauthor

Goodreads: https://geni.us/Goodreadsauthor

Bookbub: https://www.bookbub.com/profile/n-o-one

Linkedtree https://linktr.ee/n.o.one